UNINVITED

JUSTINE MUSK

POCKET BOOKS   MTV BOOKS

New York   London   Toronto   Sydney

POCKET BOOKS, A Division of Simon & Schuster, Inc.
1230 Avenue of the Americas, New York, NY 10020

First MTV Books/Pocket Books trade paperback edition September 2007

POCKET and colophon are registered trademarks
of Simon & Schuster, Inc.

For information about special discounts for bulk purchases,
please contact Simon & Schuster Special Sales at
1-800-456-6798 or business@simonandschuster.com

Designed by Carla Jayne Little

Manufactured in the United States of America

10 9 8 7 6 5 4 3 2 1

Library of Congress Cataloging-in-Publication Data
  Musk, Justine.
    Uninvited / by Justine Musk.
      p. cm.
    Summary: When Kelly Ruland's older brother Jasper returns to town a year
and a half after running away, a mysterious motorcycle gang follows him home
and causes trouble for the Ruland family.
  [1. Brothers and sisters—Fiction. 2. Family life—Fiction. 3. Interpersonal rela-
tions—Fiction. 4. Space and time—Fiction.] I. Title.
  PZ7.M97258Un 2007
  [Fic]—dc22
                                                            2007010306

ISBN-13: 978-1-4165-3827-1
ISBN-10:   1-4165-3827-5

PRAISE FOR
JUSTINE MUSK'S

BLOODANGEL

"Justine Musk is a talented, vivid writer and a voice we'll be hearing for a long time."

—Poppy Z. Brite

"[An] unusually compelling story of the supernatural."
—*Chronicle*

"Musk has created an array of fascinating characters and an intricate plot which is vaguely reminiscent of early Anne Rice."

—*Romantic Times*

"Reading *Bloodangel* is like avidly watching three separate trains race towards each other at neck break speed. . . . The excellent writing and engrossing story lines fill the mind with evocative imagery that lingers long after you put the book down."

—*Black Gate*

"Musk delivers vivid characterization of her human and otherworldly characters, delivering an action-packed apocalyptic story line full of self-discovery and empowerment. This was a thrill ride of a read, and it comes highly recommended."

—Rambles.net

For Shirley Jean Wilson
who never doubted.

ACKNOWLEDGMENTS

Thanks go to my family, Shirley and Terry and Erin Wilson, and husband, Elon Musk, for enabling my daily trips into my private worlds through all the years before publication. I am forever grateful.

Thanks also go to Maye Musk, Blackbook, John Skipp, Mark A. Clements, and the astonishing bookseller (as well as talented writer) Rob Crowther Jr.; to my agent Andrea Somberg and editor Jennifer Heddle, who have given me only good things to say about them; to Ron Bean and Lisa Litwack, for my love of cool silver things; to the urban fantasy writers in the "fangs, fur & fey" community for being an inspiring pack to roam online with; and to the storytellers at www.storytellersunplugged.com, for their wit, wisdom, and grace.

When you look long into the abyss, the abyss also looks into you.

—Friedrich Nietzsche

PART ONE

Notes from the Ride (I)

The address turned out to be a plain wooden building set back on Sunset.

The teenager, pale and rangy in ripped jeans and a T-shirt, stood on the sidewalk in a hammerfall of sun and examined the street in both directions.

He saw traffic clotted along the snakelike road. He saw clubs, dark and shut down and waiting for the night; he saw boutiques and restaurants, music stores and billboards and palm trees, hotels that seemed carved from cubes of sugar. People were lingering around an open-air newsstand, flipping through magazines, sipping iced coffee drinks.

He didn't see any of the other Riders.

He didn't see Archie.

Maybe I'll really get away with this, he thought, and opened the door and stepped inside.

The interior was sterile and air-conditioned, done in white and black, as if part of the store was just a negative of the other part. Glassed-in cases lined either wall and displayed a staggering variety of piercings and tattoo stencils. The stack of books held more work, he knew, but he also knew the designs he sought and needed would not be among them.

"Help you?"

The man who appeared behind the counter was a big, burly guy, his arms sleeved out with tattoos and his face studded and dangling with jewelry. For all that, his manner was gentle.

The youth said, "I'm looking for Cairo."

"Sorry?"

"Cairo." He heard the anxiety in his voice. Couldn't seem to hide it.

Or maybe seeming stressed-out wasn't such a bad thing. The man's expression softened a little, even as his eyes flickered with the slightest hint of distaste. "Oh," he said, "okay. You're one of those."

"Cairo's here?"

"You tracked him down, huh? I hear that's not easy, not these days. How'd you manage it?"

"Long story."

"Always is."

He led the youth toward the back of the shop. They passed a black-haired woman reclining in a dentist's chair, grimacing as the tattoo artist worked the needle along her dusky stomach. The man swept aside a curtain and they stood inside another, smaller room. There were tools and needles of varying lengths laid out on the counter, and a row of oddly glittering paints and dyes and powders. The smell in here was different, smoky and earthy, cut through with the coppery suggestion of blood.

"Wait here," the man said and disappeared through another door in the back.

The youth waited. His hands were shaking just a little. His leather jacket was in the rucksack strapped to his motorcycle; if he'd been wearing it, he could have hid his hands in the pockets. He held them in front of his eyes instead and forced them to still.

The door opened again and a different man stepped through. He looked to be in his early thirties, although the youth knew he had to be much, much older than that; he had a shaven head, muscular arms, steel rings lining both earlobes. "So," he said, his brown eyes narrowing as he looked the youth over from head to toe. "What's your name?" He spoke with a British accent, which the youth had not expected.

"You don't look anything like him," the youth said instead. "Is it true you're his brother?"

"Half brother," Cairo said.

"Your back. You don't have w—"

"No. You know, I spent a lot of time and effort trying to make him see reason. But he is what he is and he does what he does. So now I help foolish kids like you. Your name?"

"I've been—" The youth took a breath. "I can't seem to remember it. My name. Not for the last five hours."

The brown eyes turned to slits, then Cairo shrugged and turned away. "You're pretty far gone, then, aren't you?"

"But I—" Anxiety in his voice again, verging on panic. He swallowed hard, said, "I made it *here,* didn't I?"

But Cairo had said the very thing the youth himself had feared, ever since he opened his eyes to the day and reached for his name and grasped nothing but air.

"If I could make it here, then I must have—I must have some of it left, right? My soul? It's not gone completely, right?"

Cairo turned his hands into fists and tapped the backs of his knuckles together. "I'd like to help you, kid. I really would. If you could just tell me your name." He crouched a little and put his hand on the teenager's shoulder. "Convince me we have something to work with. Why don't you go somewhere and think on it for a bit? Clear your mind, and relax, and see if you can't—"

"Jasper." The name broke from his lips like a trapped bird escaping. "My name is Jasper Ruland."

Cairo straightened. He turned away toward the table that held the rows of tools, the inks and paints and powders. "How'd you learn about me?"

"Inigo."

"Huh. I heard Archie and that animal had a falling out. So it's not just a rumor."

Jasper said nothing. Waited.

"That doesn't mean you can trust him," Cairo said. "You know that, right?"

"I helped him," Jasper said.

"You did?"

"Yeah."

"Huh." Cairo studied him anew, as if forced to readjust his impressions. "That adds a new wrinkle. Maybe you could tell me about it."

"Long story."

"We've got the time. You understand this is a long, complicated process? You'll be here for many hours?"

"Yeah."

"You understand how much it hurts? And there's nothing I can give you for the pain, not now, not later?"

"I don't care."

Cairo picked up a tool. He held it at arm's length, set it down again. There was tension in his shoulders, the line of his jaw. In the same mild tone of conversation, Cairo said, as if to distract both of them, "So where will you go when it's over?"

"Home," Jasper answered, and the man moved toward him with the needle.

CHAPTER ONE

Kelly Ruland didn't know how long the animal had been watching her.

She was at the edge of the road, studying the memorial that she and her friend Nick had been working on for the past few months. After countless designs they decided on a tall wooden obelisk, which they cut and hammered together in Nick's stepfather's workshop. On two sides of the triangle, Kelly painted a portrait of each of the high school students who had died. The third side she had sponge-painted black.

Black for mourning. For the night of the car accident that had stolen so much.

Black for the abyss.

The thought came to her, unexpected and unexplained, and she jerked her head.

It was then that she saw the coyote.

At least, she thought it was a coyote. It looked a bit like

a medium-size German shepherd, sitting on its haunches at the edge of the tree line. His fur—she was suddenly certain that the animal was male—was dark tan washed through with black. His narrow head was pointed toward her, ears sharp and alert, as if there was something he needed to communicate. As if they were on the verge of a conversation.

She listened to the wind in the branches, breathed in the smell of green earth.

The coyote lowered his head, as if bowing to her.

Then he slipped into the woods.

"Nick," Kelly said.

"Yeah?" Lanky Nick Hollinghurst was loping up the side of the ravine, twigs snapping beneath his hiking boots, digital camera in hand. He'd been taking shots of the memorial from different perspectives. The sunlight was the lazy, melted-butter kind, but the sun was dropping into the horizon and it was time to go home.

"I just saw a coyote. I think."

"Really?"

"It was awesome." She turned to look at him. "Are there even coyotes around here? Aren't they only in the wilder places?"

Nick shrugged. His sandy-colored hair was cropped close against his skull, emphasizing his dramatic widow's peak. She had known him for over two years now, ever since his family had moved here from the city, and he seemed to have grown when she wasn't looking: transforming from a boy of average height and weight into this long-limbed high school senior who was taller than her father. His new haircut, and the way it emphasized his eyes, which were hazel and intense in a way she wasn't sure she'd truly noticed before, further disturbed her sense of familiarity. Some moments it was almost as if her good buddy Nick had disappeared, to be replaced by this attractive imposter. This stranger. But then she blinked, and saw her buddy again. "Good food sources for them, close to humans," he was saying.

"For the . . . what?"

"Coyotes." He glanced at her oddly.

"Sorry. Distracted."

He grinned, and for a moment seemed to know she'd been distracted by him, his own face and body.

But no, she realized. Nick was still kind of clueless that way.

He said, "What do you think of the memorial? Happy with it?"

"'Happy' doesn't feel like the word."

"I guess not." His expression sobered and for a moment there was silence between them. "Are you satisfied with it?"

"I guess."

She wanted to say something more. Something about how empty she felt now that the project was done. How it seemed in some ways like it had been only a few weeks, instead of just over a year, since a car accident killed Ronnie Patel and Kira Thatcher. They had both been friends of her older brother, Jasper.

He had had a lot of friends, once.

Her brother. Kelly wanted to say something about him. How much she missed him. He had walked clear of the accident, trudging up the sloping, leaf-littered side of the ravine just as Nick had a few moments ago. His car, a secondhand Honda Civic he'd bought with money earned working in their father's restaurant, had flown off the road and crashed into the trees below. Ronnie had been thrown from the car and broken his neck and spine, Kira died from internal bleeding en route to Selridge General. Jasper was unharmed. Not a bruise. He refused to answer any questions, seemed in shock. There was some question that night if he could even remember anything; Ronnie appeared to have been in the driver's seat, but Jasper refused to confirm even that.

And then he was gone.

He'd passed a Breathalyzer test and shown no signs of alcohol in his system—Kelly had never known her brother to drink—but rumor had it there'd been drugs floating around the rave. Ecstasy, ketamine, marijuana, GHB. Maybe he'd been tempted. Kelly doubted it. Her brother had been against all that stuff. But he disappeared from the hospital before agreeing to be tested for drugs of any kind.

He had left a single message on the family voice mail:

Don't try to find me. You can't.

"He's obviously guilty and ashamed," people whispered. Or sometimes they didn't whisper it behind Kelly's back, said it straight to her face, even yelled it at her once, after a high school football game, Kira's best friends still in their cheerleader uniforms, one of them picking up a rock and throwing it at Kelly, narrowly missing her. Then and now, Kelly didn't see how that rumor could be true. *Ronnie* had been in the driver's seat, and everyone in contact with Jasper that night had described her brother as sober and coherent. But he had gone from being the boy with everything going for him—including early entrance to Harvard—to the notorious runaway in just a handful of hours, and Kelly suspected that even his friends had taken his absence as an admission of guilt.

So had she. She still didn't think he was guilty of the accident—didn't see how that could be possible. If his actions were those of a guilty man—and she had to admit they sure seemed like it—then he had to be guilty of other things. She just didn't know what they were.

Except for: not a single letter, postcard, phone call, e-mail, instant message. She had idolized him all her life and he knew that, and now there was only this fat dark nothing where her brother had been. This space marked Missing Person. And he had done that to them, to her.

She often dreamed they were in a room together and she was yelling at him.

His face wasn't on the memorial, but, for Kelly, his presence was all around it, all through it. She had made it, she realized suddenly, for him.

She mentioned the coyote at breakfast the next morning.

Kelly's father was chef and co-owner of a restaurant in downtown Selridge; because he often didn't get home until past midnight, breakfast had become the official family meal. Since Kelly's pregnant mother had been confined to bed rest a couple of weeks ago, they brought breakfast up on trays and ate in the master bedroom, sitting on or around the king-size bed. The little red-haired dachshund, Mojo, lay on her bed in the corner and waited to be tossed bits of sausage.

"A coyote?" Hannah said, absently stroking her belly. She had declared that she was going to do bed rest in style: she wore silk pajamas and the lariat necklace Robert had given her for their last anniversary; she did her hair in a chignon every morning and had a friend drop by every week to give her a pedicure, since she could no longer reach her toes or even see them over the still-growing mound of her belly. Kelly knew there were two little babies evolving in there . . . but at the same time found it difficult to believe they were actually going to insert themselves into her life, in all their bright, squalling ferocity. "This omelet is lovely, Robbie."

"I made it," Kelly said.

"Well done, you."

Robert glanced skeptically at his daughter. "It might have been a dog. Some kind of shepherd."

"It wasn't a dog. It was a coyote. It looked right at me. For a moment I almost thought he was going to start talking to me. It was bizarre."

"I have to go," Robert said. He was rolling up his shirtsleeves, revealing the sea snake tattoo from his days in the navy. "I've got vendors to deal with." He touched Kelly's shoulder. "Have a good day at school."

"Right."

"Give my regards to the talking coyotes. You think they sing and dance, too?"

He chuckled to himself as he left the room. Kelly said to her mother, "Does he actually think he's funny?"

"As long as he cracks himself up—which he does—I don't think he cares." Hannah shifted her position on the bed. She had already arranged the day's reading on the pillow beside her: she was switching between a biography of Goya and a book of short stories by Joyce Carol Oates. "We go together like hard and soft," Kelly's father liked to say whenever their friends remarked on what an unusual couple they were: the ex-sailor turned chef, the refined college professor. "Like day and night. Like caviar and white bread you buy at the convenience store." Kelly didn't think her parents were such an odd pair. They had cut into each other over the years. You saw how they fit.

Hannah said, "They have an interesting role in mythology, you know. Coyotes."

Sometimes Kelly blanked out when her mother went into professor mode, thought of other things—the latest handbag she wanted, what TV show was on that night, when she'd next be able to get into the city—but she found herself eager to talk about this. "Yeah. The moment was very . . . it just seemed very . . . it seemed more than ordinary."

Hannah yawned. "They're tricksters," she said. "Always up to no good."

Mojo trotted over to the side of the bed. Kelly picked her up, snuggled her for a moment and kissed the top of her head, then put her on the bed beside Hannah. Kelly said, "Didn't that poet guy write a book of poems about a coyote?"

"Poet guy?"

"The husband of the *Bell Jar* chick. When I dropped by your class once you were talking about him."

"Sylvia Plath. Don't say 'chick.' It's demeaning." Kelly rolled her eyes, which her mother pretended to ignore. "And you're talking about Ted Hughes. He wrote about a crow, not a coyote, but both those animals are often considered to be tricksters in various mythologies, so I can see how you would—"

"Trickster," Kelly said. "Sounds like a good name for a band."

"Maybe you should look it up."

"Maybe I will."

"You do that, my curious child," Hannah said, and in that moment Kelly could almost believe she was still the kind of girl who looked things up, whose grades never equaled her brother's but, when combined with her athletics, signaled a scholarship at a decent university. Kelly pulled away from her mother. Hannah's eyes darted to a framed photograph on the wall—all of them together, Hannah and Robert and Kelly and Jasper, the pretty happy family—and away again. The cheer in her voice sounded forced. "What are you girls doing tonight?"

"Oh . . ." She hated lying to her mother, but she had also gotten good at it. "They're going to force me to watch that Colin Farrell movie. Morgan will show off whatever designer things she bought in the city. And I'll make caramel popcorn while they pretend to help."

"And the Diamond Dog."

"What?"

"I'm no idiot, Kelly."

No, Kelly thought. *You're just . . . depressed. Detached.*

But Kelly couldn't blame her, and the truth was she was grateful for her mother's pregnancy for a couple of reasons. The first, and most important, was that it gave her mother a purpose and focus other than her missing son. The second was because, between her mother's high-risk pregnancy and her father's work schedule, which had only intensified since Jasper's disappearance, Kelly found herself left to her own devices in a way she had never been before. As long as she kept her grades mildly respectable, which she could do if she showed up enough and paid enough attention—although even that was becoming more and more of an effort—she had trust and freedom.

"We won't stay out past curfew," Kelly said. This was true, but not for the reason she was about to give her mother: "That's when the freaks and creeps come out anyway."

"Good to know. Although I'm not sure I want to know how you know that."

"I'm a good kid."

Her mother opened one eye, then closed it again. "No one suggested otherwise."

The conversation appeared to be over, but Kelly lingered. She wanted her parents to leave her alone, yet she also wanted them to pay more attention to her. It was a contradiction, she knew, and she didn't really understand it. She gave her mother's belly a pat, saying hello to the little creatures inside, and left the room.

A short time later, Kelly went online:

. . . as their name suggests, tricksters love to play tricks on other gods (and sometimes on humans and animals). The trickster figure crosses both physical and social boundaries—the trickster is often a traveler, and often breaks rules.

What kind of rules? Kelly wondered. She sighed and shut down the computer. She was reluctant to let go of the whole thing. It had been like a moment of magic in her life, lifting her out of herself, and now she had to accept the boring banal reality of what it had actually been: just a stupid animal.

She heard a car honk outside. Her friend Amy Garcia would be in the driver's seat and Morgan Sutton would be up front beside her. Amy would want to see the memorial, but Kelly didn't feel ready to share it with them, not yet. The memorial felt too private, like something shared between her and Nick.

Or maybe Jasper.

Kelly sighed, and pushed her hands through the dark angled layers of her hair. It was amazing how somebody's absence could burrow into your chest and gnaw the bones there.

Amy honked again.

As she walked down the driveway, Kelly was suddenly

conscious of the oaks and maples scattered across the rolling green of their yard, of the hedges that marked off their
property. The hedges needed trimming, the grass needed
cutting. Their yard was always a little wilder than their
neighbors'. She imagined places for a shaggy tan-black body
to crouch and hide, imagined animal-gold eyes tracking her
as she cut across the lawn to where her friends were parked
curbside.

She slid back the door and got inside. Amy and Morgan had the alt-rock station turned up loud. They had gone
shopping for school supplies—cute jeans, hooded cardigans,
maybe some notebooks and pens while they were at it—and
were picking up Kelly on their way back to Morgan's place,
where they would have the house to themselves to get ready
and plot out their night. "Hey, sexy girl," Amy said, flashing
a crooked grin. She was a leggy cinnamon-skinned girl with
her dark wavy hair caught back in a head scarf. "Took your
sweet time." The Lincoln Navigator actually belonged to
Morgan's mother, who allowed Morgan and her older brothers to share it. But somehow Amy always ended up in the
driver's seat, which none of them felt the need to mention
to Morgan's parents.

Kelly's eyes flicked to the trees again. *Stop obsessing,* she
told herself, but that steady yellow gaze lingered on in her
mind. *It was just a stupid animal.*

CHAPTER TWO

"Party!" Amy yelled as the three of them trooped into Morgan's bedroom. Amy leaped over to Morgan's iPod and speaker system and pressed Play. "Did you download that new song by the Killers?" she asked. Before Morgan could respond, Amy did a pirouette in the middle of the floor—Amy had been taking ballet and jazz lessons for close to ten years now—and whirled on Kelly. "I have something for you," she declared. *"Pour vous!"* And then she was unzipping her red knapsack, taking out two bottles: one of tonic water, one of gin. "And this," Amy said, holding up a lime and a small knife. "Because details are very important. Morgan, get some glasses . . ."

"If my mother ever caught us—" Morgan said.

"As long as you don't breathe on her or fall down drunk, you'll be fine. Besides—" Amy assumed her grown-up tone. "—if you are to drink, I'm sure your mother would prefer that you drink inside the home. That way she knows where you are. C'mon, Morgie, you need to live in the moment. Carpe diem. We could all die tomorrow."

"That's unlikely," Morgan said.

"This is Kelly's favorite drink. So we must drink in honor of Kelly."

"Why?" Morgan said.

Amy shrugged. "Why not?"

Kelly grinned, accepting one of the red plastic cups that Morgan brought out from the adjoining bathroom. As soon as the alcohol touched her tongue she felt a quick twist of guilt. She'd been feeling it a lot lately. Not just for lying to her parents, or sneaking around, or engaging in the kind of behavior that she used to think—when she was younger and much more judgmental—was only for burnouts and losers. For some other reason she couldn't put it into words. It was more of a feeling. Like she was betraying something, or someone. Betraying, maybe, the person she was supposed to have become.

Lighten up, she told herself. *Forget that girl.* Everyone else had.

Morgan's bedroom made Kelly think of a hotel suite. In addition to her own white marble bathroom, Morgan had a private balcony overlooking the hills. As Amy searched through the selections on Morgan's iPod, fragments of one song after another winging out from the speakers, Kelly slid open the glass door and stepped outside.

The air was mild, but when the breeze swept her face Kelly felt the cool undertones that signaled a new season. She sipped her gin and tonic. It tasted cool and sharp and limey. In the past months she and Amy had experimented with whatever alcohol Amy could slip unnoticed from her parents' extensive liquor collection or persuade one of her many cousins to buy for her. They'd gone through scotch, tequila, rum, vodka, Kahlúa, getting seriously sick after a night of mixing and drinking white Russians. Kelly had managed to pass off her hangover as the stomach flu, although she had the nagging suspicion that her mother hadn't believed her, merely lacked the energy to press the matter further. Whatever. There was nothing to worry about, she was just in some kind of experimental phase.

The night swept through the tumble of hills.

"I asked you a question," Amy called from inside. "Didn't you hear me?"

"What?"

"I said how come you and Nick haven't—" There was a vibratory buzz as Amy's cell phone went off and Amy jumped to her feet. "Gotta take this," she yelled gleefully, "'cause we're gonna *roll* tonight!" She moved to a corner of the room. Morgan was sitting on the edge of the couch, a small brown-eyed girl with blonde hair falling around her pale face. She smiled at Kelly. They had been best friends all through grade school, had survived the slow rise and sudden fall of Kelly's popularity, but now Kelly and Amy were drawing close and Morgan could feel herself being squeezed out. Kelly knew this and sometimes felt a little guilty. She smiled back at Morgan. "Good outfit," Morgan said approvingly, and Kelly glanced down at herself to remember what she was wearing. A long blue cami belted over distressed jeans, cowboy boots, silver bracelets stacked on her wrist. All things that Morgan had helped her pick out.

"I have a good stylist," Kelly said.

Morgan looked pleased.

Then Kelly said, "Has someone moved into the Heath place?"

She was looking at a hilltop at the far edge of view, at the vague shape of the house that sprawled there. Lights glowed and flickered . . . and Kelly thought she could hear the distant sound of music, despite the distance and the heavy bass thumping out from Morgan's room. But when she listened again, it was gone. "There's somebody up there," Kelly said.

"I noticed that, too." Morgan joined Kelly on the balcony. "The goth kids go up there to play vampire games."

"I don't think it's them."

"You think somebody is actually living there?"

"Doesn't it seem weird?" Kelly said. "The way the lights are kind of . . . flickering and moving like that? It's like the house isn't staying completely still."

But Morgan was tracking a different line of thought. "You know, when we first moved into this stupid McMansion? I didn't want this room, because I didn't like this view. It's like, every time I find myself looking up at that house, I feel like that house is looking back into me. You know?"

"That's because you're high-strung."

"Shut up."

"Every town has a house like the Heath house," Kelly said. "A handy source for urban legends."

"But—" Morgan was about to say more when Amy called them back into the bedroom.

"We're set." Amy was grinning, draping herself across the bed and striking a pose. "He's got the stuff. We're meeting him at nine sharp beneath the oak tree at the corner of the parking lot."

"This is pretty dicey," Morgan said. "I don't like it."

"But you like what it does for you. So give me your money."

"I don't like this part. We could get caught. Jason and Samantha and Tiff—"

"Were burnouts. And morons. They were doing it at *school,* for Chrissake. *We* are not morons." Although Kelly had to wonder. Was the line separating them from people like Jason Morris and Samantha Julavits really so solid as Amy made it out to be? As if picking up Kelly's thoughts, Amy made a face. "We're just nice suburban kids gone slightly astray. You have no skill for being bad, Morgie. No matter how much I try and try to teach you. I might have to give you a failing grade, Morgie. You might have to go to summer school."

"What if somebody sees us? What if—"

"Have you seen *the guy*?" It was how she referred to her connection; Kelly didn't know if it was because he genuinely kept his name a secret from her or if Amy just enjoyed the sense of mystery. Kelly guessed the latter. "You haven't seen the guy so you don't know. So I will explain. The guy looks like a young Republican who goes to Bible study every week. The kind who marries young so he can get laid without feeling guilty after. Not the type who draws suspicion."

Kelly wrapped her arms around Morgan's shoulders and kissed her on the cheek. She smelled of baby powder. "Soon," Kelly promised, "you'll be feeling really good. Really, really good."

"I know that," Morgan said. "I just wonder if it's worth it."

The pills were a dark purple color, with an image of a little stick figure with wings stamped in the middle. Six hits of ecstasy in the little baggie, fifteen dollars each, which Amy informed them was an excellent price. Three pills for tonight and three to keep in reserve. They never did more than one a night, taken in halves. "Here you go," Amy said, handing the first halves out to her friends. They were sitting in the Navigator in the parking lot behind the club. Amy passed around a bottle of water. Kelly felt the weight of the pill on her tongue, the awful bitter taste. She felt the twist of unease she always felt at this moment, when she still had the chance to refuse. But it's not like this was cocaine, or heroin, or any of the hard drugs that turned people into total losers. She washed it down quickly. She closed her eyes. *What if it was bad stuff? What if I die? What if I have a bad trip and feel cockroaches crawl all over me or something?* And behind those questions, the other one that kept nagging her, wouldn't leave her alone: *Why do I keep doing this?*

Amy said, "You know the hardcore way of taking E? You put it up your butt."

"You're kidding." Morgan wrinkled her nose.

"You *stick* it up your *ass*," Amy said, grinning directly into Morgan's face, "and let it sit there and dissolve. It hits faster that way. That's how they do it in Ibiza."

"Duly noted," Kelly said.

"Maybe next time we should—"

"No," chorused Morgan and Kelly, and they looked at each other and laughed.

"Such wusses," Amy chided, sliding the door open and jumping out.

It was an all-ages night at the Diamond Dog, so they didn't have to worry about who was guarding the door and whether they could flirt or con their way past with their pathetic fake IDs. Which took some of the drama and excitement out of the evening, Kelly thought. But the inside was already filling up, kids swarming the dance floor and crowding the bars, and the music came like waves breaking over her. She felt a glow start in the pit of her stomach and radiate through her body. It was too soon for the ecstasy to be taking effect; maybe this good feeling was from the gin she'd been drinking earlier.

Or hell, maybe she was just feeling good to be alive, here with friends, moving out onto the dance floor.

And then, to make it even better, she saw Nick standing off to the side with a couple of his friends, smart boys who weren't exactly cool but weren't quite geeks, either. Nick wore a gray V-neck sweater over a white T-shirt and jeans and boots; he was the tallest guy there and looked older and more confident than she knew he was. The other boys barely managed to smile at Kelly as she approached.

Once, she would have made an effort to be friendly to them, because she didn't want anybody thinking she was standoffish or a bitch, but now she no longer cared. If they couldn't be polite to her just because she had once been popular—and therefore part of an established social order they had taken it upon themselves to despise—that was their problem.

But when Nick turned and saw her his face lit up and his body seemed to open toward her. A delight went through her, deeper and better than any pill could give her, because it was real. It wasn't a trick of chemistry. For a moment she couldn't speak. He smiled, gave a little awkward shrug, said, "Dance?"

She nodded.

She always felt good on the dance floor. She wasn't as impressive as Amy, but she knew how to let the rhythm get inside her and move her around and she knew she looked all right. Nick shuffled from side to side and mostly kept the beat. The next song slowed a little and Nick put his arm around her, drew her toward him so he could yell in her ear, "I wanted to talk to you!"

"About what?"

He said something she couldn't make out clearly. It sounded like, "I think we should go out," blurted out in a rush, but she wanted to make sure she had the words exactly right. She yelled at him to say it again. She saw him pause, take a breath. She stepped in a little closer. But instead of leaning down to speak into her ear again, he touched her face, sweeping his fingertips along the edge of her cheekbone. "How did you get these?" he asked and she knew he meant the scars.

She frowned. "I told you," she said. "Didn't I?"

She could see him thinking back. "Dog attack?"

"Why are you asking me this?" She meant now, on the dance floor.

He shrugged, gave a sheepish little grin. And she understood he was stalling, asking her this question in place of his real question.

Hell with it, she thought, and stood on tiptoe to yell in his ear, "I think we should hook up." She rocked back on her heels. He was smiling. Warmth opened up inside her chest and she didn't think the drug had anything to do with it. *Hell with it,* she thought again, and rocked up on tiptoe again, leaning into the warmth and the light soap-scented musk of him, and kissed him on the mouth.

A different feeling came over her and she stepped back.

She saw his eyebrows lift, saw his mouth form her name. But she turned and made her way off the dance floor and fell against a pillar. She closed her eyes. *It will pass,* she told herself. *It always does.*

"Kelly?"

The voice sounded like an echo, traveling across a vast distance, even though Amy had appeared right beside her, Nick coming up behind. Amy's face was a study in concern and possibly fear—as if she was afraid the pills they'd swallowed were toxic in some way, because you never knew, did you? You always took a gamble when you got something off the street, whether it was a hot dog or a drug; some gambles were just bigger than others. But no, Kelly wanted to explain. This feeling had nothing to do with the drugs. It would have happened anyway. It was as if a coffin made of shadow had closed around her, sealing her off from her friends, taking her away from the lights and energy of the club. She felt cold— she was shivering now—and everything sounded muffled, as if buried under three feet of snow. *It will pass. It always does.* The darkness was squeezing her now, like a series of clammy hands roving all over her body, pressing and pressing on her chest. *It will pass,* she told herself, and took a long slow breath—counting *one, two, three, four*—and held it, then slowly released it—*one, two, three, four*—*it's all in your mind,* she told herself, *you know this.* But the darkness was slipping inside her now, mixing with her blood, pumping through her body, her heart and brain—her soul—

It will pass.

But behind that voice of calm clear rationality piped up another, different voice, brittle as a twig about to snap: *You are dying.* She looked for Amy and Morgan, for Nick, and although she knew they were all in front of her she could no longer see their faces through the darkness and she couldn't hear them at all. She was locked inside a box that was spinning away from everyone she loved. *Maybe you're already dead.*

And then, just like that, the box opened. The darkness lifted out of her, receded. "—should call the paramedics," Nick was saying and Kelly held up her hand.

"I'm fine," she said.

"You sure?" Nick said and Morgan said, "Kelly—"

"This has happened before," Kelly said. "It's kind of an—an anxiety disorder." She felt herself growing hot with embarrassment. She wanted to get past this moment as fast as possible.

"You should drink some water," Nick said. "When was the last time you ate anything?"

"I guess it's been a while," Kelly admitted.

"Look. I'm gonna go next door, get you a burger and a Coke, okay?"

"That's really nice of you, but—I'm fine, Nick. Really."

Nick shrugged. "Look, it's no problem. The music here sucks anyway."

As they watched him wind his way through the crowd to the main entrance of the club, Morgan said, "Wow. He's really nice."

"Are you kidding? He's trying to get laid," Amy said. She glanced at Kelly. "Although I do think he, like, really likes you. He's kind of, you know, guileless. Isn't he? He is without guile. That's what's so cute about him."

"Without guile?" Morgan said.

"He's obvious about it," Amy said.

"But Kelly's kind of obvious about it, too, so it's not like he's risking anything."

"Would you not talk about me like I'm not here?" Kelly said.

"We weren't," Morgan said, sounding slightly offended.

Kelly pushed her hands through her hair. "I need some air," she muttered. She angled her way through to the fire exit and pushed out to the back parking lot.

It was a relief to get free of the club. The air, a little cooler now, swept her face, and she breathed in the distant scent of burning leaves and the closer one of cigarettes. Heels tapped along cement, laughter rose and faded, as a group of girls wound their way through the rows of glinting cars. There was no one else in the lot. "Kelly?" Amy said, falling in beside her. The girls got into a car, doors slamming. Music pounded out from the club. Kelly took a deep breath. Amy said, "Are you sure it wasn't—that what happened back there wasn't—because of the stuff we took?"

The feeling had nothing to do with the drug.

Kelly shook her head. "It's happened before."

The feeling was why she *took* the drug.

"You never told me that," Amy said.

"It's not something I want to talk about."

Morgan said, "Kelly, have you seen a doctor about this?"

"Yeah, I had chest X-rays and stuff. There's nothing physically wrong with me." It's just . . ." She hunched her shoulders, let them fall. "Anxiety. Stress."

From Amy: "Did you at least get some Xanax out of it?"

"No," Kelly said sharply. "I don't need stuff like that."

"God, calm down. I was just asking."

Morgan said, "Have you talked to, you know, a shrink?"

"I went three times, after Jasper left, but I didn't like the guy and my father doesn't believe in that stuff anyway and so we decided I had better ways of working it out. Like in the gym."

"What did your mom think? She seems like someone who—"

"She wanted me to find a new shrink," Kelly said, "but she was outvoted."

"Kelly," Morgan said. She was twisting her hands together. "My mother's best friend has an anxiety disorder. I saw her have an attack once. It looked . . . different . . . from what was happening to you in there."

"How so?" Although she wasn't sure she wanted an answer.

"She was hyperventilating and stuff. But you—you looked like you weren't breathing at all. You looked like you were just shutting down, and your *eyes*—your eyes had this strange expression, like there was nobody behind them for a moment, like the real you was going somewhere else."

"You mean right out of my head," Kelly said flatly.

A woman walked past them, smoking, and Amy stepped forward and bummed a cigarette. The woman let Amy use her lighter. "Yeah, Morgie's right. It was pretty freaky," Amy continued. "Nick wanted to call nine-one-one."

"Maybe you should have called the people in white coats instead. You make me sound like I was—crazy." What was the word? "Catatonic."

"But it was just for a minute," Amy said, grinning. "The minute passed." She took a drag off the cigarette and shook back her hair. "Hey," she said. "Do you feel it?"

And even as she was speaking, it was as if a warm and gentle hand ran across Kelly's scalp. She felt her body relax and her mind brighten. She took a long cleansing breath and the parking lot, the cars, the street beyond, the red brick wall: everything clicked into sharper focus. She looked around with new interest.

Morgan's eyes were bright; Morgan was feeling it, too. "It's time to go back, right?"

This was their rule, and in the handful of times they'd done ecstasy before, they'd managed to adhere to it. They would not be high in public. Morgan insisted on this. She would only do E with them if they could hang out in the safety and privacy of her house, where, as far as Morgan was concerned, nothing bad could happen. She wasn't just paranoid about getting caught (three kids had been discovered taking ecstasy in the woods behind the school last spring, were arrested and promptly expelled), she was anxious and paranoid about getting anxious and paranoid, and she wanted no cause to freak out. As it turned out, having the run of Morgan's house—the hot tub, the pool, the huge flat-screen TV—turned out to be pretty great when you were hyped and happy on E. They could form their own cozy little world, talking intensely for hours, and the night seemed like it would last forever even as it passed in a blink. And the truth was, Kelly appreciated Morgan's cautious nature. Without Morgan, she knew, she and Amy ran the risk of discovering a whole new level of trouble, and deep down Kelly knew that was not what she wanted. She was a good kid, after all. A little partying with her best friends didn't change that. Dropping out of soccer and softball and drama club didn't change that. Stashing a bottle of gin in her room so she could sneak the occasional—okay, more than occasional—little nightcap to help her get to sleep didn't change that, either. What was the alternative, after all? Shrink sessions? Xanax? Please. She was not one of those pampered, whiny, neurotic suburban teenagers whose so-called mental health depended on a dozen different prescriptions.

But she needed to get away from that *feeling*.

That feeling of a coffin closing around her, darkness descending, spinning her away from everyone and everything she'd ever loved.

She realized her hands were still trembling. She pressed them together to make them stop. She really was starting to feel better. It was like a dark grim weight had been lifted off her shoulders and she could breathe again.

She rolled her shoulders, luxuriating in the feel of the movements. From somewhere down the street she heard the rev-rev-rev of a motorcycle.

"We should go now, while I'm still okay to drive," Amy said.

"Let's go," Kelly said. She walked out into the parking lot. Behind her, she heard a soft thump and clattering sound. Morgan swore. Kelly glanced over her shoulder and saw Morgan crouched on the pavement where her handbag was spilling out half its contents. Amy was helping her gather, plucking an eyeliner pencil from a crack in the pavement.

"Hey—" Kelly said, or began to say, because that motorcycle sound was getting very loud. She looked over to see a single headlight cutting down the street, passing beyond the maples and oaks that edged the sidewalk, before approaching the far corner of the Diamond Dog's parking lot. She saw the dark shapes of more motorcycles streaming out behind the first, engine sounds layering to a deep and oily roar as the bikes turned one by one into the lot.

"What the hell—" Kelly said.

The roar filled her ears and the bikes were all around her: weaving through the parked cars, crisscrossing the sweep of pavement. Headlights slashed apart the shadows and tossed glare in Kelly's face. She was forced to squint, shielding her eyes with her hand. Vague details of the riders: black leather, tattered jeans, longish hair blown back, lean bodies, strange faces. She heard someone—Amy—call out from behind her, but it was impossible to make out her words through the drone of the engines. The smell of gasoline laced the air. Headlights kept roving over her so that she had moments of being blinded which intersected with glimpses of the bikes—flashes of chrome and steel and neon color—not the burly Harley-Davidson type but sleek, streamlined machines that seemed melded to the crouched, shadowed bodies of their riders. The engine sound was very loud now—had any noise ever been louder?—and for a moment Kelly thought it would just go on forever, that sound would never end—

Except then the roaring softened into a steady growl. Now she could hear laughter, as well, but it sounded wrong—too high-pitched, coming from too many places at once—and there was a hollowness to it that made the back of her neck turn cold. It was laughter that didn't sound fully human. Light continued to shine in her face and she had to put up both hands to block it. It was like being onstage and staring into the white sun of the floodlights, knowing you were being watched but unable to see who was watching—except when she'd been in school plays she had felt powerful and now she felt stripped and exposed. She wanted to yell out something defiant, like one of those heroines you saw on TV. But her voice wasn't there. Her throat was dry.

Slowly, she turned around, squinting through her fingers. She couldn't see Amy and Morgan. All she saw were the lights, and the backlit suggestions of motorcycles, the long lean riders who straddled them, their gaunt and shadowed faces. They had formed a circle around her. She sensed the collective weight of their gazes like a blade aimed at her throat. She was no longer breathing.

One of them called out, "Is that her?"

"Yeah," another voice said, "that's her. The sister."

She tried to look in the direction of the second speaker but the engines revved up again, the circle dissolving, the bikes turning and streaming away. She stood like a figure trapped in ice. As the bikes slipped through the parking lot and faded down the street, a hard cool silence settled in their wake.

"Oh God," Kelly said. Amy and Morgan were beside her and Nick was cutting toward them across the street, gripping a paper bag from the fast-food place. She wondered if he, too, had seen the convoy of bikes; he must have heard them, at least. She cleared her throat, made her voice as tough and scornful as she could: "What the hell was *that* about?"

"Those guys," Morgan said. "They're not from around here."

"You think?" Amy's voice was thick with sarcasm, but it softened as she turned to Kelly. "What did they say to you?"

"Nothing."

"But I heard—"

Sister. But she wasn't ready to think through the implications of that. What that might mean. Because that went into an impossible direction. Her heart felt high and rapid in her chest.

Enough of this, she thought.

She hadn't come out tonight for strange anxiety attacks and a herd of jerks who thought they were cool because they could ride motorcycles without falling down. Tonight she was supposed to have fun. Feel good. Find some release before another school year slammed down a new beginning. The night was still young. It wasn't too late.

"Nothing," Kelly said again, and from the tone in her voice her friends knew to leave it alone.

Just before Nick reached them with the food she already knew she wasn't going to eat, she whispered in Amy's ear, "Where's the stuff? We've got more E, right?"

"Yes," Amy said uncertainly. "In the car. But—"

"I want more."

CHAPTER THREE

Amy and Morgan were crashed out in Morgan's room. But Kelly was still buzzing, restless, hyped-up. She'd taken more E than either of them—she could tell from even Amy's disapproving glance that she'd taken too much—and although she wasn't as high as she'd been just a little while ago (*and good,* said a voice, *because you were too high, and you KNOW that, it was STUPID STUPID STUPID to take that second pill, and you KNOW that*), it would be a while before she came down completely. When she looked at herself in the mirror, the blue of her eyes was nearly swallowed by the black of her pupils. It altered the look of her face. She almost didn't recognize herself.

She thought, *Maybe that's not me at all.*

She wanted her own room, her own bed. She decided to walk: it was only a couple of miles, through cool and quiet streets. It was Jasper who liked to walk, for miles, who had quit the competitive pressures of track partly to go hiking instead, often by himself, in the woods and out through the town. "Clears my head," he had told Kelly. Once home he would go into his bedroom, blast music, and write in his notebooks for a while. Maybe when you were as brilliant as everybody said Jasper was, that's how you had to treat your head: like a storing house that needed to be swept clean on a regular basis. Usually Kelly thought walking was boring—if you wanted exercise why not do a martial arts or dance class, or ride your bike?—but the idea of walking through a mostly sleeping world right now seemed appealing.

She stepped outside. The grass looked soft and inviting. On impulse Kelly removed her shoes and walked across the lawn. People should go barefoot every day, she decided, when she felt a sting in her right heel. She picked up her foot and examined it. A sliver of glass was embedded in her sole. Gingerly, she picked it out and put her foot down in damp grass—

—and the coyote was sitting right in front of her.

Bargains of blood and sinew and bone, he said, and Kelly was not surprised that he could talk, had even expected it. Because this must be a dream, right?—and animals talked in dreams all the time. *Other bargains, soul-deep bargains, of tricks and illusions and lies. They must not be kept. Yes?*

"What the hell?" Kelly said.

Love and fear in your brother. For you. He made his mistake for you. You must take back the sacrifice. Or both sister and brother will reel through all that is lost. The coyote tilted his head. *Sometimes the dark place,* he said, *is the right place. Yes? You must reclaim. There must be a reclaiming. Or the soul of your brother is as lost as all the other lost things, the car keys and ball pens and women and men.*

"Jasper?" Kelly said. "What do you know about Jasper? Where is he?"

Archie is coming. He's already here.

And then he was gone.

Kelly stood there, her shoes in her hand, feeling self-conscious and stupid. *I just had a conversation with a coyote.* "I can wake up now," she said to no one in particular. Her foot stung where she'd picked out the glass but held her weight okay. She looked back at the white faux-colonial façade of Morgan's house. She didn't want to go back inside. If she wasn't going to wake up yet, then she might as well dream about walking home, through the still-sleeping streets.

She spent the next two days curled in bed, feeling like she wanted to throw up and cry. *I'll never do E again. Never, never, never.* She told her mother she was fine: just one last lazy stretch before the first day of school. Hannah gave her a suspicious look but said nothing. Her father was busy with a private party at the restaurant and didn't see her at all.

She thought about the coyote a lot. Had it been a waking dream or a full-fledged hallucination? Was the ecstasy screwing up her mind? Was she going crazy? She felt that black-coffin feeling reaching out for her—like a monster made of emptiness, grabbing her up in empty hands, toward an empty mouth.

She was her father's daughter. She was a tough kid. She wasn't the kind of girl who cried easily, or at all.

Those hours, though, she came close.

CHAPTER FOUR

She went through the first morning of school feeling comfortably numb. In fact, that was the song on her iPod she kept playing over and over: "Comfortably Numb," not the original Pink Floyd version that Jasper kept forcing her to listen to, insisting it was one of the greatest rock songs of all time, but the recent version by the Scissor Sisters. *New year, new start,* she told herself, doing her best to work up some enthusiasm. *Try not to screw up too much.* She didn't know if the bleakness inside her was an aftereffect of the E or if the bleakness was always there and the E just managed to override it for a while. She wasn't stupid. She knew the stuff didn't fix anything in her life. She didn't need an episode of *Degrassi* to teach her that. There was a voice in her head that kept taunting her: *Such a loser. Such an idiot. You peaked at fifteen and it's all downhill from here.*

When she reached her locker between first and second period, Nick was waiting for her.

She saw him as she rounded the hallway corner. He wasn't looking at her, he was speaking with a friend and she had a moment to take in the long lanky length of him, the habit he had of tucking his chin just a little into his neck as he talked, so that he looked up in a way that made him seem both sheepish and bemused. She was eager to see him, had found her mind circling around thoughts of him all morning. But when the friend moved away and his gaze shifted toward her, she didn't know what to say to him. Had absolutely no idea. She thought of the last time he'd seen her—collapsing at the club, like she was either totally wasted or totally neurotic or both.

"Hey." He seemed a bit stiff, not like the easy laughing way he'd been talking with his buddy. Was he feeling awkward too, or was it just her?

"Hey," she said.

They compared schedules and exchanged small talk about kids and teachers. And then he rubbed his hand across the top of his head and squinted down the hall and she sensed what he was about to say and wanted to avoid it. "About the other night," he said. "You know. At the club."

She said, "Can we just not talk about it?"

He was still looking down the hallway, as if something extraordinarily fascinating was taking place at the end. "Not talk about it?"

"I wasn't exactly at my best."

And now he looked back at her. "Were you rolling?" Asking her point-blank.

"I—" She thought about lying. Would have lied, maybe, if he had been anyone else. "Yeah."

"Kelly. I don't mean to sound like a prude or anything—I mean, I'm no angel, I kind of dabbled when the divorce was happening and stuff—but that's also kind of why I know—I mean, from personal experience—that you should be careful."

"I am."

"It might not seem like a big deal, but—"

"I said I know. Don't lecture me, okay?"

He looked down the hallway again.

"So," he said, and his voice didn't sound as friendly, "so that stuff you said to me on the dance floor? Do you even remember it?"

"Of course I remember it."

"But you weren't exactly sober, right? You were just feeling really good and warm and cuddly, right?"

Something in his tone, and in the way he'd lectured her, made her feel even more depressed and prickly.

"I guess," she said.

He took a step back, raising his hands a little, his notebook in one and cell phone in the other. "Okay," he said. "Don't worry about it. Later, okay?"

"Nick," she said and sighed. "It doesn't mean that I didn't mean—"

"It just would have been better if you— Ah, shit. Just forget it. Just take care of yourself, okay? I'm kind of worried about you."

"I'm fine," she said. "Like I said, it wasn't my best night."

"Whatever. Like I said. Later."

He moved inside the flow of students and was gone.

She wasn't up to facing the whole cafeteria scene. She assigned herself the task of decorating her locker. She never made a production of it the way some kids did, but the barren metal in its ugly yellow color was depressing the hell out of her. She taped up some postcard reproductions of her favorite Gauguin and Matisse paintings, then arranged a cluster of photographs beneath a little mirror. Pictures of her friends, of Mojo on the beach staring distastefully at the lake, and finally a picture of Jasper from two years ago, before the accident.

Kelly stared at the last, unable to look away.

They had gone into the city together, just the two of them, with no other plan but to bum around and see where the day took them. It was her reward for finishing the list of fifteen books that Jasper had dared her to read, stuff she would never have picked up otherwise, from Robert Heinlein's *Stranger in a Strange Land* to Ayn Rand's *The Fountainhead*. He had been giving her a list like that every year since she was ten. In the picture, he was sitting on a rock in Central Park, beneath low-hanging tree branches, sun and shadow sifting over him. His light brown hair was windblown, elbows on the knees of his jeans as he leaned forward, smiling at her through the lens of the camera. It wasn't a big smile, but the warmth and affection was real. When Kelly saw the picture for the first time, peeking inside the sleeve of photos as she stood outside the drugstore, she went back to the counter to get a duplicate. If she ever lost this photo—she had a talent for losing things—she wanted to be sure she had another.

A group of laughing shrieking girls passed behind her, jostling her back to the here and now. She was going to be late. She gathered up her binder and pencil case and shut the locker door with a *clang* that went right through her skull. Since she had taken the E she had slept without really sleeping, and she'd been walking around with a headache and an unsettled feeling in her stomach. Just thinking about the year that stretched before her now, everything she was expected to *get through,* let alone *accomplish,* made her want to sit down in the middle of the hallway and give up.

She opened her locker door again and looked at Jasper's photo. Then she thought, *Bastard,* just because it seemed easier to be angry. You could hide a lot of things—hurt, for one, and betrayal and abandonment, for another—behind something so glaring and flashy as anger.

Enough of this. She was sixteen, after all, not six, and she needed to find her goddamn science class.

She made her way to the west wing of the building and checked the room number on her schedule. When she found the door and reached to open it, she had a flash of *something not right,* but before she had a chance to examine that feeling more closely she was stepping into the classroom—

It was empty.

Dust motes swirled inside the sunlight slanting through the open windows and the smell of chalk and floor cleanser mingled with the fresh earthy breeze. The desks were lined up in perfect rows. Printed neatly on the blackboard was the line "I ALL ALONE BEWEEP MY OUTCAST STATE." There was a small glass sphere on the teacher's desk, like one of those paperweights you shook to make it snow inside. This one didn't have any snow, but it contained a little scene: Kelly saw woods and a road, and for half a second she thought she saw a little figure moving—

"May I help you?"

She whirled. She could have sworn she was the only person in the classroom, except now a man was standing in the far corner. He was tall and thin, with a shock of bright blond hair that nearly touched his shoulders, and as he walked toward her she noticed his cheekbones, so high and sharp inside his face they seemed about to cut through skin. He wore a black jacket with a frayed lapel over black-and-white–striped pants. He didn't look like any teacher she had ever seen before. He was tossing something in his hands that flashed in the light. It was the paperweight, Kelly saw. Except how had it gone from the desk to his hands . . . ?

Kelly said, "I'm looking for biology?"

"This would not be it." He smiled and she did her best to smile back. "I'm Mr. Archer." He offered her his hand.

Something tugged at her mind—a bit of memory, of dream—but was gone before she could grasp it fully. "Um," she said. "Kelly."

"Lovely to meet you, Kelly. You like biology?"

She shrugged. She was looking at the sphere in his hand. Again, she thought she saw trees, a car, and small figures— she thought she saw them moving—

But then his fingers moved across the glass, covering what was going on inside, and she forced herself to remember his question.

"I like math and art," she said.

She should be on her way to class, she knew, not standing here making conversation. She was so late. But something in this man's gaze caught and held her. His eyes were a light golden brown, the color of caramel.

"Not so fond of literature? Poetry?"

"God, I get enough of that stuff from my mother. She's been preaching it to me her whole life." Kelly reflected a moment, then shrugged her shoulders. "I don't understand why so much of literature has to be in, you know, code. Why can't writers just say what they mean? Instead of using symbols and things to make everything difficult?"

"They don't do it just to be difficult. You like your truths to be self-evident. Plainspoken."

"Of course. I mean, doesn't everyone?"

"But life is not always like that, Kelly Ruland. Sometimes the truth is not so obvious. You need to find it behind and between things. People pretend to be talking about one thing when they're really communicating something else. So it's important to always look beneath the surface. Always, always, always." He smiled at her, pale hair glinting in the slant of sun, and said, "Us, for example. What do you think we're really talking about, you and I? Beneath the surface?"

"I . . ."

Was he seriously asking her this?

She glanced around the empty classroom.

She should leave. She knew she should leave.

Yet still, his eyes, his pale blue eyes—although hadn't they been a different color just moments before?—held hers, and she couldn't look away. There was such kindness in those eyes. Wasn't there?

"I could tell you things," he said and now she was starting to feel twisted and weird inside. "I could give you answers to some of the questions burning inside you. About your brother, for example."

"What?" She stared at him. "What did you say?"

Mr. Archer smiled. He was tossing a green apple in his hand and she blinked at it—where had that come from? What happened to the paperweight? He raised it to his mouth and bit. The moist crunch sounded loud in the silence of the classroom. "Think about it," he said. "Think about the kind of truth that you're prepared to handle. We'll see each other again, I'm sure."

She was conscious of him still standing there, still smiling at her, as she fumbled for the doorknob and spilled into the hallway. Couldn't get out of there fast enough.

It wasn't until later in biology class, as Ms. Gregory assigned the first reading exercise that got everybody groaning about the homework they already had, while the teacher only gave them a pitiless smile, that she remembered the way the strange teacher addressed her. *But it's not always like that, Kelly Ruland.* But she was pretty sure she had only told him her first name, not her last.

"I don't know, Kelly," Morgan said as she reapplied pink lip gloss and slipped it back into her small purse. They were walking down the corridor toward the heavy glass doors. "It sounds just a little too . . ."

"Too what?"

"Too creepy and weird to be true," she said.

"Don't be naïve, Morgan," Amy said. "There are pervs all over the place."

"I didn't say he was a perv," Kelly said uncomfortably. "That's a pretty nasty label to just slap on a person."

"Dude, you didn't say he *wasn't,* either."

"It's not like I was getting that kind of vibe from him, but it was weird. There was something about him that didn't seem . . ." She stopped in the middle of the hallway to think of the right word. But the right word seemed to be eluding her and all she could think of was, "He didn't seem right. Natural. I mean, he seemed *unnatural.*"

"Maybe he's a vampire or something. That would be so cool. I want to meet him," Amy decided. She stopped right in front of the doors, forcing the flow of kids to part around them. "Let's go see him right now."

"Amy!" Morgan clucked her tongue.

"I want to see this Mr. Archer for myself. Since he's a

new teacher at my school and he might be a perv and all. It's like my mom always says. Forearmed is forewarned." Amy raked dark curls out of her eyes. "Kel, where was his classroom?"

Kelly looked at Morgan and shrugged. Morgan was sticking out her lower lip a little, a habit of hers that Amy liked to make fun of from time to time, but Amy's idea didn't seem like such a bad one. Kelly was no doubt exaggerating the whole incident without realizing, making it into something that it wasn't. Her mother was often going on about how memory couldn't be trusted; people were constantly sifting back through their private histories, revising and rearranging them to fit the stories they wanted to believe about themselves, accurate or otherwise. Kelly had blundered into the wrong classroom, she was still shaking off the ecstasy hangover that was no doubt screwing up her perceptions, and the new English teacher had simply made conversation with her as part of his effort to get to know the student body. Maybe he was a bit creepy, but that didn't mean he was—what was the word she had used moments before?

Unnatural.

Which is exactly what Amy would tell her, after she'd seen Mr. Archer for herself.

"This way," Kelly said and led her friends back through the hallways. She made a left turn and walked in the direction of the gymnasium, then stopped. "It was here—"

Morgan and Amy were looking at her with puzzled expressions.

"Don't think I really need to point this out," Amy said

cautiously, "but this, you know, *this* is the girls' *bathroom*."

As if to prove it, the door swung open and three girls dressed for field hockey bumped their way past them.

"I could have sworn it was—" Kelly looked around her. "Then maybe it was over here—" She walked down the corridor, then walked back. "But it was here," she said, and made no attempt to mask her bewilderment. "I swear it was. I remember it being opposite the orange lockers—"

But she stopped herself and stood in the hallway, breathing in air weighted with cleaner plus traces of the different colognes that had accumulated through the day. She flashbacked to one oddity after another. The man's eyes changing from brown to blue. The way he'd already seemed to know her. The little figures that had seemed to move inside the round glass paperweight—which must have been a trick of the light, or a trick of her mind—

Morgan said, trying to be helpful, "Maybe it's the next classroom over?"

"No, because that's the biology lab. That's the room I was trying to find."

Morgan said, "Are you all right, Kel?"

"I'm *fine*." How many times did she have to say this? "I'm *fine*, I'm *fine*, I'm *fine*."

"Whoa." Amy held up her hands. "Easy, girl."

Morgan said, "You know, what happened to you the other night—the anxiety attack, or whatever—did it, um, maybe it happened to you again today? Maybe it, like, distorted your perceptions—"

"No."

And beneath the surface of Morgan's words, Kelly knew, other questions crouched: *Are you losing it, Kel? Are you falling apart more and more? We've been worried about you since your brother ran away, you know that, right?*

Kelly tightened her hold on the straps of her knapsack and took off down the hall. She heard her friends calling her name, heard the mingled sound of their footfalls following hers. Students loitered at their lockers, or sat cross-legged on the floor with their backs against the wall, or gathered at the benches beneath the skylight in the lobby. Kids who would have called out to her in the past and waved her over to join them, kids who once tried to suck up to her on a daily basis, now ignored her. She'd been part of the popular group but now she was disinvited. Uninvited. She'd seen it happen to others who had fallen or been pushed from the group, but hadn't really believed it could happen to her.

She waited at the counter until Mrs. Wallace had finished explaining some kind of schedule mishap to the new student ahead of her. As the boy left, he cast Kelly a quick, friendly look of commiseration, as if to say, *This place is crazy, huh?* Kelly fidgeted with the straps of her knapsack.

"Yes?" said Mrs. Wallace. "Yes, Kathy—?"

"Kelly."

"Of course. Kelly. I'm so sorry I forgot your name." The little woman blinked behind her oversize glasses. "The first day, you realize. I'm fried."

"I wanted to ask about the new English teacher."

The secretary gave her a blank look.

"The new English teacher," Kelly said again. "Mr. Archer?"

"I'm sorry, dear, I really have no idea—Linda?"

A woman's head popped above a partition. "Yes?"

"Is there a Mr. Archer at this school who teaches Spanish?"

"English," Kelly said.

"Is there a Mr. Archer at this school who teaches English?"

"No," the woman said and popped back down.

"He's tall," Kelly said and it seemed to her that her voice became touched with the slightest hint of desperation, "and thin, and has whitish hair that's kind of longish—" She held a hand at her shoulders, indicating the length. "He's kind of unusual-looking—striking—he'd be hard to forget—"

"Maybe he doesn't teach English here, maybe at Rexford?" She was referring to Rexford Collegiate, the private school a mile or so down the road.

"Right," Kelly said. "That must be it." She stepped back from the counter.

"Anything more I can help you with, Kathy?"

Any reports of strange classrooms that just disappear from existence right after you've been in them? Kelly thought but did not say. She laughed out loud, but did not feel amused; she felt, instead, a kind of scrabbling in her chest.

"Kathy, dear, you look a little . . . ashen. Are you feeling—"

"I'm fine," Kelly said. "I'm great."

A trick of the mind. *Her* mind. How many times could

you do E before it damaged your mind? She hadn't done it *that* much . . . had she?

Just a couple of nights ago I was having a conversation with a coyote.

But no, that was a *dream*. She had *dreamed* that.

She went out into the hallway. Morgan and Amy had their backs to her, were chatting up a couple of boys who had strayed out of basketball practice. And suddenly Kelly knew right in her gut that she couldn't deal with any of them right now.

She turned and walked quickly in the opposite direction, then pushed through the front doors and started to run.

CHAPTER FIVE

Her bedroom window overlooked Robson Avenue, a wide winding street lined with cracked sidewalks and towering oaks and sugar maples. She was trying to study—get her homework done on time, get the year off to a good start—but the view was distracting. Victorian houses, some of them in better shape than others, sat back on sprawling shadowy lawns. Soon the trees would be stripped bare. Soon there would be snow and ice.

No one in the street now, as late afternoon cycled into early evening and the shadows of the trees reached across uneven sidewalks. A squirrel made a mad dash from hedge to tree. Kelly looked back to her textbook . . . when she caught it again: a sleek dark shape flitting through the edge of her vision, down in the street below. Except this time it didn't seem like a squirrel.

Except the street was empty.

She thought back to the afternoon—the teacher that

wasn't supposed to be there in the classroom that didn't seem to exist—and felt her chest tighten. Kelly glanced back to her notebook, where she saw she had scribbled the number 432 over and over again in the margins. She frowned—432 wasn't the answer to anything—and turned her pencil on end and erased it. She was going to figure out the value of X because math, at least, was predictable and logical and made perfect sense . . . Kelly scratched in her notebook. If Y= −4, then X would equal—

432, she thought again. But no, that was all kinds of wrong. Yet she couldn't help thinking it: 432.

What the hell. She'd finish this later. She turned to her creative writing assignment. She was supposed to write a personal essay about an important person in her life. What about the important person who was *not* in her life? She tapped her pen against the spirals of her notebook. Hannah had taught her that instead of thinking and worrying yourself into creative paralysis, you should just write whatever came into your head without judging. Something about left brain versus right brain. You could go back and rework it later. The important thing was to get it down.

So she wrote:

When I was born, and my parents brought me home from the hospital, my older brother Jasper put books on my face. This isn't as bad as it sounds. They were his favorite books in the world. I kept crying—I guess the whole "birth" thing had turned out more traumatic than I'd expected—and Jasper kept asking our parents how he could make me "happy." Since his favorite books made him happy, I guess piling them on my face seemed like a good idea at the time.

Books came up again in our relationship some years later. Unlike Jasper, who was already reading by the time he hit kindergarten, I was slow to learn. It wasn't until second grade when words finally "clicked" for me, when printed stuff started making sense. It was like waking up one morning in a foreign country and finally being able to speak the language. But by then kids were already calling me stupid, and I had started to think of myself as stupid. So I just assumed I didn't like reading. Besides, I was too busy practicing back hand-springs with my best friend Morgan and also playing soccer and baseball. Because that kind of stuff I knew I was good at.

When I was in third grade I told Jasper how frustrated I was because when people found out I was his younger sister they expected me to do as well in school as he did. And nobody does as well in school as he does, or if they do, they don't make it look as easy as he does. "And besides, I'm not smart," I told him. "Yes, you are," he said. "You share the same genetics as me, so why wouldn't you be? You just need to read more. Reading is key." When I asked him why this was, he just shrugged. "School is easier when you read a lot," he said. "But I don't like reading," I said. "Sure you do," he told me, "you just don't know what it is you like to read. Real reading isn't the same as reading the stuff they shove down your throat in

school. I'll take you to a bookstore and help you pick out
a book you'll really like. You'll see. . . .

"Kelly!"

Her mother's voice sounded from down the hall.

Kelly made a show of sighing, even though no one was
around and she was glad for the excuse to shut her notebook. Her mother was propped against the headboard, reading the Goya biography; at Kelly's footstep in the doorway
she looked up and said, "Could you take Mojo out?"

"Mojo doesn't look like she wants to go out."

"Mojo's been curled up on this pillow for the past eight
hours," Hannah said. "I think it's high time she visited a nice
patch of grass."

Kelly scooped up the warm velvet curl of dachshund,
who gave the smallest of growls as she felt herself disturbed.
"Don't cop that attitude with me, little beast," Kelly said.
Mojo licked her hand.

"The great existential question of a dachshund's life,"
Hannah mused, "would be something along the lines of,
'Am I comfortable enough? Can I be *more* comfortable?'"
She chuckled to herself. Kelly didn't always get her mother's
humor, but she was glad to see Hannah in a reasonably good
mood.

Pausing in the doorway, hugging Mojo's long body against
her chest, Kelly dropped her gaze to her mother's belly beneath the white comforter. Hannah always had one of her
elegant, long-fingered hands resting atop it, as if keeping
everything in place, as she read or ate or watched DVDs, or

talked to her husband or daughter, or one of the students
or teaching assistants or girlfriends who were often dropping by, bringing books and magazines and the homemade
chocolate almond bark she liked so much.

Mojo yawned.

"Anything I can get you, Mom?"

"Some tea might be nice, if you should find yourself in or
near the kitchen."

"Sure."

At the bottom of the stairs, Kelly put Mojo down and
started to open the door. Mojo cracked open a massive
yawn and shook her head, ears flapping, as if resigning
herself to the inevitable if temporary fate of cool dark air
and damp grass. Usually Kelly didn't bother with a leash.
Their yard was not fenced in, but Mojo rarely strayed far
from couch or bed. She would saunter onto grass, squat
her hind section, kick uselessly at the dirt, and hurry back
to the door.

But tonight for some reason, maybe the snake of unease
that now seemed to live inside her permanently, Kelly found
herself opening the closet door, taking down Mojo's leash
from its hook, and snapping it onto the little dog's collar.

They stepped out onto the front porch. Kelly had just
hopped down the stairs to the walkway when she heard
Mojo growl in the back of her throat.

"Mojo." She was too startled to say anything other than
the dog's name. Mojo broke into a series of staccato barks
and raced ahead of Kelly until the leash yanked her short.
She continued to bark: bullets of sound that ricocheted

down the street, until a neighbor's Lab started howling in response.

Kelly saw grass, trees, shadow, the hulking forms of other houses: lit-up windows signaled life inside, but outside there was darkness and quiet. "Mojo," she said. "Mojo!" She yanked on the leash, pulling the dog toward the door, but Mojo could set a whole new standard for stubbornness when she wanted to and she wanted to right now. She planted herself in the grass. Kelly was afraid that if she kept pulling she would hurt the little dog's neck. She tried to pick her up but Mojo read her intentions and danced away. "Mojo," Kelly said again, "come here, you—"

She heard, then, the light rhythmic trot of an animal down the street.

A shaggy dog was headed toward her, passing between shadow and streetlight, nails clicking lightly along the pavement. But Kelly was suddenly aware of what she didn't hear. She didn't hear the jangling of dog tags—sounds of domestication and ownership—as the creature edged out of the shadow and into a cone of pale yellow lamplight on the other side of the street from Kelly.

Her breath caught.

Not a dog. Of course not.

The coyote held himself still in the light, beneath the arch of streetlamp. He sat neatly on his haunches and aimed his head in her direction.

Mojo stopped growling. She whimpered, then fell silent.

Kelly and the coyote stared at each other.

She had to check herself. She was awake and completely

sober and this was not a hallucination. This was not a dream. This was doing homework on a school night, taking the dog out to pee.

The coyote still did not move and neither did she. Her chest hurt and she realized she wasn't breathing: afraid the tiniest gesture would scare it away, end the moment.

"Hey," she said quietly. She remembered what her mother had said, what she had read the other day on the computer. *Trickster. Traveler. Boundary-crosser.*

Where did you come from? she wanted to ask him. *What boundaries did you cross to come here, to me, now?* It was silly, of course, just to think of such questions, to think of asking him any questions at all, because no matter how strange or beautiful or magical this moment seemed, the animal so still within that pale yellow glow, while her neighbors' houses hunkered down in silence in the crisp September dark, it was, in the end, just a coyote, just an animal like any other animal, about as likely to answer questions as Mojo was to do simple calculus—

"Did you talk to me the other night?" she said. Her voice carried in the clear evening air. She hoped there was no one around to hear her. "I know it sounds really stupid, but do you have something to *say* to me?"

The coyote tilted his head.

And then:

"Kelly," a voice said, as a tall figure in jeans and a hooded sweatshirt stepped in front of her.

She shrieked. She couldn't help herself: It was that sudden, that unexpected; the person seemed that unfamiliar.

Until she looked again.

He said her name again.

And she couldn't speak at all.

"It's me," her brother said. "It's me."

He lifted both hands a little, as if approaching a nervous horse, as if to say, *See? No tricks. Nothing strange. It really is me, your brother, after all this time . . .*

He had grown very thin. The sweatshirt hung loosely off him. His hair was the same sandy shade she remembered but longer now, falling in his eyes and shoulders. His face was different, as if the weight loss had taken a blade to his features, carved out a new gaze from those blue eyes. They were hollowed and shadowed in a way they had never been before.

She spoke slowly. "Jasper?"

"I think," her brother said, and she saw that he was swaying on his feet, "I think I need to lie down—"

He took a step and stumbled. Instantly she was there, providing balance and support, his arm heavy on her shoulders as they made their way up the driveway. Mojo trailed behind them, her leash dragging along the pavement—Kelly realized she had dropped it. She also realized that Mojo was barking, had probably never *stopped* barking.

Then they were inside the house: the warm air and overhead light and lingering smells of garlic and tomato from the pasta dinner Kelly had cooked: all of it safely enfolding them as she kicked shut the front door. She helped her brother into the living room, where he pushed himself away from her so that for a moment he was standing, looking at the pale yellow walls and cream-and-blue furniture and abstract, Asian-inspired watercolors above the fireplace. "Wow," he said. He looked at the books in the bookcase, the upright piano that nobody played anymore. "Holy shit. I guess I'm home."

He smiled at Kelly, then collapsed like a house of cards onto the couch. He closed his eyes. In a moment he was faintly snoring.

"Oh my God," Kelly said. She clenched her hands and pressed them against her mouth. "Oh my God, oh my God, oh my God." She wanted to shriek and yell as loudly as she could but settled for mumbling into her fingers. She backed out of the living room, staring at her brother the whole time, and was jumping around the hallway when her mother's voice came from upstairs:

"Kelly?"

A floorboard creaked overhead. She felt her eyes widen. Was her mother getting out of bed? "Mom," she called out, "you're not supposed to—" And then she was flying up the stairs.

Her mother was sitting on the edge of the king-size bed, both hands placed against the beachball crest of tummy. Her face and neck were flushed. "Kelly," she said, "what the hell is going on? What was that I heard downstairs? Why—"

"Mom—"

"—was Mojo barking like a mad thing? The neighbors—"

"Mom, you won't believe it—"

"—are going to take out a gun and *shoot* her if she keeps yapping like that—"

"Jasper," Kelly said in a fierce exhalation of breath.

"What?"

"Jasper. He's here. He's back."

She saw Hannah's lips shape her son's name, but silence hung in the air for a very long moment before Hannah said, cautiously, as if not yet daring to believe: "Your brother? My son?"

"My brother, your son!"

Hannah raised a hand and touched air. "You wouldn't say that if it's not true. You would never dream of doing that to me."

"He's downstairs!" Then: "Mom. No—"

Hannah was on her feet, moving into the hallway. Kelly trailed after her, saying, "Mom, you're not supposed to be out of bed—and you are *not* supposed to go down the stairs—Mom, you could *bleed*—"

"I'm going to see my son," Hannah said, and her voice closed out all possibility of argument. Kelly could only hover around her as she took the steps one at a time, gripping the railing with her left hand and lowering herself down each one, until her bare, pedicured feet touched the ground floor.

And then she was in the living room, kneeling beside the couch, and she said, "Oh my God," and in that moment the bones inside her face seemed to collapse, her mouth falling open. Tears slipped from her eyes. "My baby, my firstborn baby, my son . . ." and then her voice went very soft as she kept muttering things that Kelly couldn't hear, as she stroked back Jasper's hair so she could kiss his forehead again and again. Then she was saying, "You're back. You came back. You came back."

"Yeah," said Kelly. "He came back."

Jasper stirred, opened his eyes, smiled sleepily up at her. "Hi, Mom," he said. He propped himself up on his elbow to get a better look at her. "Holy shit," he said, "you're so . . . you're so . . . you're so freaking *pregnant*."

"Twins," she said. She was laughing.

"Twins," Jasper said, and he touched her belly as if he thought she might be putting him on and it would turn out to be a secret cushion. He looked just as stunned as Hannah had, moments ago in her bedroom.

Hannah grabbed Kelly's wrist. "You'd better call your father."

It turned out the restaurant was having a bad night. They were overbooked again. Then one of the line cooks had snapped, tearing off his chef's jacket and throwing it in the manager's face. It was an in-the-weeds situation, when everything hovered on the thin narrow edge of falling apart, and Robert was doing everything he could to get the place through it before customers started walking out. It took an hour for Kelly to get the message to him, and another forty minutes before he burst into the house. He barely acknowledged his daughter and his wife. His gaze frantically sought out his son.

By then, Jasper was sleeping deep and hard, as if he had discovered true sleep for the first time in months. Kelly tried to imagine what kind of life he'd been leading outside her own personal context of home and town, but came up with nothing. Both Hannah and Kelly had taken up positions in the winged chairs to either end of the sofa, watching Jasper sleep as if he were the most riveting movie that had ever been filmed. "You know there actually was a film once that showed a guy sleeping for hours," Hannah was saying when Robert finally broke in on them.

"Son," he said. "Son."

Jasper stirred, as if responding to the sound of his father's voice, but didn't wake. Kelly had thrown a red wool blanket over him and now it slipped partway to the floor, revealing part of Jasper's back and one arm.

"How did this happen?" her father asked. He was hovering over Jasper, reaching out as if to touch him but drawing back at the last moment, as if Jasper might prove an apparition that would vanish on contact. Noting the wetness of her father's eyes, Kelly explained how she'd taken Mojo outside, how Jasper had just appeared in the driveway. How he had said her name.

"How did he get here?" her father said. "Did someone drop him off?"

"He said he walked."

"Walked?"

"He took a bus," Kelly said, "and walked here from the station. That's, what, three miles?"

"Look at him." A gruff tenderness in her father's voice, but also that note of criticism that seemed permanently embedded, especially where his firstborn was concerned. "He looks like hell. He doesn't look well."

Hannah murmured something Kelly couldn't hear. Hannah's endless, soundless crying was starting to give Kelly a small case of the creeps, seeing the tears stream down her mother's face like that, the rest of her so still and quiet, her gaze transfixed on her lost-and-found son. Kelly found herself thinking of those statues that were said to weep real tears or bleed real blood. Every now and then Hannah would murmur, "I knew he'd come back. I knew it. I knew it," but Kelly suspected her mother was lying. She hadn't known. No one had known except Jasper, and maybe not even him.

After discussing the matter in hushed voices, even though Kelly figured a train could tunnel through the living room and still fail to wake her brother, they decided to leave him where he was. Hannah wanted to stay, but the chair had not been designed for a woman seven months pregnant with twins and already Hannah looked cramped and pained and exhausted in a way that made Kelly increasingly nervous. "I'll stay right here, Mom," Kelly said. "I'll keep an eye on him. He's not going anywhere. When he wakes up I'll bring him straight to you."

"All right," Hannah said, and she ran a hand across her face, smearing her tears, and reached out to once more stroke the hair back from Jasper's forehead. She allowed her husband to maneuver her up the stairs. Kelly listened to their footsteps overhead.

She had meant exactly what she'd said. She was afraid that if she took her gaze away from Jasper, even for a minute, he would disappear, and she would wake from a dream too vivid and real. She sat in her chair, wrapped in the blanket she had brought out for herself, and watched the streetlight work its way through the gauzy curtains and form patterns of light and dark across her brother's body.

His right sleeve had been pushed up to his elbow, exposing a deeply tanned forearm dusted with light brown hairs. And . . . were those hints of ink, traced deep into his skin, extending just past the edge of the sleeve? Kelly got off her chair, crouched by her brother. She had a whole new take on the phrase *sleeping like the dead,* even as Jasper's chest rose and fell in the rhythm of the living. She gently pushed and tugged back his sleeve. On Jasper's arm was an intricate network of barbed and swirling lines, criss-crossing the tight curve of his bicep, running up underneath his shirt. Some of it was done in a dark ink; some of it in a pale silver; some of it in a light blue that actually seemed to glitter, like the body paint she and Morgan used to decorate their faces and shoulders one Halloween when they dressed up as fairies.

It was a breathtaking arabesque of a tattoo, in shapes and colors she'd never seen on skin before. She didn't even know you could do that on skin.

And then—

One of the shapes seemed to move. Seemed to lift itself ever so slightly, its section of the design turning three-dimensional, and then shift into a new position. A rippling ran out along the intersecting lines, racing across Jasper's skin.

She thought, *Didn't see that. No, I didn't.*

The altered part of the arabesque then seemed to sink back into her brother's skin, as if this has been the intended design all along.

I did not. She found it hard to complete the thought, as if her mind was trapped in a hurricane and struggling to move. *See. That.*

Hesitating, she reached out and brushed the section of the tattoo that had . . . changed itself. Seemed to change itself. Because stuff like that could not happen.

Trick of the light. Trick of the mind.

My mind. Which I'm obviously losing.

All she felt beneath her fingers was the warmth of her brother's skin.

Her gaze flicked upward.

Jasper's eyes were open and staring.

She rocked back on her heels and lost her balance, banging against the edge of the coffee table. "Hi," she breathed. She felt exposed, as if caught trespassing.

"Hey," Jasper said. He pushed himself up into a sitting position, his hands bracing himself against the edge of the couch. His hair, fine and silky like hers, hung tangled around his face and he pushed it back with one hand, yawning, looking spaced and groggy. He seemed oblivious to the exposed tattoo, although he nonchalantly tugged down both sleeves. She couldn't stop staring at his face. "Hey, sis," Jasper said, and she felt herself drawing forward as if on invisible strings, putting her arms around him, burying her face against his shoulder. He smelled both soapy and musky, as if his last bath had been a washing up in front of a public bathroom sink. He put his arms around her and held tight. She felt folded into him, into the newly stripped-down economy of his body. She fought against tears. She didn't want to be like her mother, who was allowed to cry because she *was* the mother. Kelly was the sister who knew to hang tough.

"How are you?" Jasper was saying. "Are you okay? All this time, Kel—have you been okay?"

She laughed a little, and wiped at her nose. "You're asking *me* that? You're the one who's been through hell. Looks that way, anyway. No offense."

He moved a little away from her so that he could look directly into her face. "I'm serious, Kelly. I need to know."

"I'm not the one who was in that car accident," Kelly said. "I'm not the one who—who's been living on the streets or, or whatever it is you've been doing—"

He made a small gesture with his hand, cutting her off. The focus, she understood, was to be solely on her. She was puzzled—this night of all nights was about *him*—but flattered by the depth of his attention. She said, "I've been here, Jasper, living . . . you know . . . living this nice cozy middle-class life." She realized she was biting down on her thumbnail.

Had he ever been this soft-spoken before? She didn't think so. "I was just wondering if . . . if you'd felt like you were being . . . disrupted . . . in a way you couldn't really explain to yourself—"

Then something in her face made him say, "Little sis?"

He reached out for her and she felt herself start. "Kel," he said, "are you okay? Are things okay?"

"I'm fine," she said automatically.

Disrupted.

Can't explain why.

The words seemed to catch so much of what she'd been feeling recently, seemed to put such a fine and precise edge on it, that it was like getting cut. It was too sharp, it stung, and she instinctively drew back. There was something shadowy, disturbing, behind that word. *Disrupted.* She didn't want to go there. She turned to other emotions instead.

"Well, *you* were gone."

He registered the note of harshness in her voice. "I'm sorry," he said simply. "For everything."

She forced herself to stop biting her thumbnail, but then immediately bit down on the nail of her pinky. "I'm not mad at you," she lied.

"Sure you are. And it's not like I can blame you."

"What *happened* to you? Where have you been?"

He looked away from her, rocking forward a little, streetlight skating along the edge of his profile. "That's a really good question," he said. "I'm still trying to figure that out."

"Christ," she said. "What kind of answer is that?"

He looked back at her and laughed. But she had the urge to scream. She had spent so long daydreaming about this moment and now that it was really truly here, she couldn't seem to make it right. Everything she wanted to say was backed up inside her, a vague amorphous mass she had no power to articulate. She stared at this person—who seemed so coiled in on himself, even in the simple act of sitting there on the couch—who both was and was not the brother she remembered. All she had to do was tilt her head and see him in a different cast of light, from a different angle, and he was a stranger.

But then he said, "Hey," and the sound of his voice made the stranger step back, revealing her brother again. "You know what I was thinking about?"

She shook her head.

"How I made you cry when we were little kids," he said. "How I used to torture you."

"You didn't really torture me," she remembered. "Just my dolls."

"Yeah, well, from the way you screamed and carried on, it was the same thing. Which I never understood, because it wasn't like I really saw you playing with them—"

"I collected them. I liked organizing them into different displays. And one day you chopped off all their heads and stuck them up around the house—"

"Forks," Jasper said. "I put some of their heads on forks."

"And Mom's students came over for one of those fireside poetry things and thought you were such a little psycho."

"Actually, no," Jasper said. "I told them you did it. And they started talking about how subversive and liberated you were, at the tender age of nine, taking this icon of traditional femininity and deconstructing it all around the freaking house. Something like that. Anyway, it seemed like a good idea at the time."

"Dad made you give me money for new dolls—"

"Yeah, the money I made raking leaves. I hated raking leaves."

"—except I decided I'd grown out of them."

"What? You acted so traumatized."

"Yeah, because that was my job as little sister. Then I went and bought some CDs. So it worked out really well for me. What are you going to do now?"

He seemed a bit jolted by the abrupt shift in topic. "Sorry?"

"What will you do now? You know Mom and Dad will get up in your face about it. Your golden future and everything."

"Maybe not so golden anymore."

"You could get it all back if you want."

"If I want it. If I ever really wanted it." He dragged his hands across his face. "God, Kelly, I can't think that far ahead. I'm just happy to be here, you know? I wasn't sure I'd get back here. Believe me on that."

She touched his knee, gave it an awkward pat. He grabbed her hand, squeezed it hard, and then let go. The gesture left her breathless. The old Jasper never would have done that.

Then their father came into the room with a celebratory bottle of Dom Perignon in one hand and champagne flutes dangling between the fingers of the other. "Let's do this down here," he said, pouring them each a glass, "so your mother won't get jealous." Robert lifted his flute and said, in that put-on theatrical manner he used to disguise real emotion, "To the return of the prodigal son!" They clinked and drank and trooped upstairs to be with Hannah on her king-size bed.

As fatigued as he seemed, Jasper was the one who directed the conversation, keeping it focused on the unborn twins in Hannah's belly. Hannah talked about the process of in vitro fertilizations in the same open, fascinated way she discussed art or literature. After describing the process to Jasper in more graphic terms than any of them would have liked, she said, "We were very lucky. We only had to go through it twice."

"I didn't even know you wanted another—" Jasper said, then stopped. As if he knew that statement couldn't lead anywhere good.

Kelly formed a response in her head: *This was Mom's way of dealing with the loss of you.* Maybe that wasn't entirely, completely true . . . but true enough. It wasn't the first time Kelly had thought this. She had never spoken it aloud. She didn't want to be misunderstood; she didn't mean that you could trade in one nearly grown son for two brand-new babies and come out even. It was more about making that kind of emotional pain . . . survivable, in some basic sense.

And beneath those thoughts ran something else that Kelly didn't like looking at too closely, that made her feel twisted and wretched inside. If all those trips to the fertility clinic and dollars spent and needles injected were, in part, to help Hannah through the absence of her firstborn . . . where had Kelly been in all this? Hadn't Kelly been enough, on her own, to give her mother a reason for pushing through the pain of all the not-knowing surrounding Jasper's absence?

Maybe the twins would have happened anyway. If Jasper left or if he stayed, maybe, where the unborn Rulands were concerned, it wouldn't have made a difference until *after* they were born.

She didn't want to dwell on these thoughts anymore. "So where did you go, anyway?"

He moved back a bit, as if the question had been a punch. Kelly realized too late that this had been the subject everyone had been avoiding, like people commenting on the color of the curtains while an elephant sat in front of them.

"Where did I go," Jasper said and hunched his thin shoulders. "Everywhere, I guess. We rode everywhere. Canada for a bit. Mexico."

"Without a passport?" Robert said.

"This guy I was with— You have to understand," Jasper said, but his voice was flat as a floorboard, as if he didn't expect them to understand anything, "about this guy. How the normal rules of things don't apply to him. Not exactly."

One of Robert's shaggy eyebrows went up. "So who is this guy, *exactly,* who gets to stand outside of the rules of things?"

Jasper stared at his father for a moment and Kelly noticed how little father and son truly resembled each other. Jasper was long-limbed and fluid where Robert was broad-shouldered and husky and several inches shorter; Jasper was fair-skinned where Robert was olive. But they had similar eyes. Blue eyes. Kelly had that same color. But father and son had a similar quality in their gazes—something fierce and hard, Kelly thought now, something that wouldn't bend easily. No wonder they had always seemed in conflict, clashing over one little thing after another, disagreeing, it sometimes seemed, just to disagree. For the principle of it.

"Yeah, he's bad news," Jasper said quietly. "But it doesn't matter now. He's gone. Him, his friends. We parted ways."

"How'd you get involved with this person in the first place?"

"In the beginning he seemed like my friend." Jasper frowned. "That's not right. Not my friend. Like my only option. It was the night of the car accident. I was coming out of the hospital and they were already waiting, they had a bike for me . . . all I had to do was get on it and—ride."

Hannah said, "I didn't know you knew how to even ride a motorcycle."

Jasper laughed. A strange, sharp laughter. "Neither did I."

"So these people were your friends?" Robert pressed. "You knew them from before? This was prearranged?"

"No, Dad. It wasn't like that. It was—an impulse thing. I was out of my head. It was—"

"Your only option?"

"It's hard to explain."

"These people were your friends?" Robert said again. His forehead was furrowed in that way that meant he was fighting to understand, to see this from Jasper's point of view. "Just explain to me how—"

"Dad. Like I said. They're nobody's friends," Jasper said. "Give me some credit, okay? I'm not that stupid."

"You want *me* to give *you* credit when you were the one who—"

"It doesn't matter," Hannah said. "It doesn't matter now. The past is the past. It was a very difficult time for us all and the important thing is that we're all healthy and well and together. Back together. Family unit made complete. Am I right?"

She was looking at Robert as she said this.

He nodded and smiled and squeezed her shoulder. "Of course you're right," he said. "You're always right. That's why I married you."

Hannah turned to her son. "Those people you fell in with," she said. "I don't doubt they were predators. People who consider themselves above the 'rules of things' generally are, in one sense or another. And you were— You were vulnerable. I mean, we all get vulnerable, but you—that night—what happened . . ." She sighed and took a moment to blow her nose. "Kira and Ronnie," she said. "But not you. Thank God."

"I know, Mom," Jasper said. "We don't have to talk about this anymore."

"Yes. This is a new time." Hannah touched the high, taut swell of her belly. "We let go of what's in the past. We move forward as a family."

There were nods all around, murmured agreements. Kelly noticed the tension in her father's face, his arms folded across his chest. Then he hugged Jasper in a way he rarely hugged anyone—and never any male—and held his son against him until Jasper pounded him a couple of times on the back and pulled away, suddenly unable to look him, or anyone, in the eyes.

When Hannah's face took on the look of exhaustion and strain again, Robert said they should call it a night. Kelly followed her brother into his old room, wanting to talk more, but Jasper collapsed like a falling tree across his bed and once again became lost in a slumber that was deep and untouchable. Kelly got a blanket from downstairs and spread it over him. She even tucked it in along the edges of his body, like their mother had done when they were little kids, as if extra snugness equaled protection.

She let her eyes roam around the room. One wall was taken up floor to ceiling with bookcases and books were lined up two deep, filling every inch of the space, spilling over into stacks beneath the windowsill. No one had touched any of it. The opposite wall was taken up just as thoroughly with music—a little bit of everything, including classical, but mostly dance and electronic. Jasper's stereo and DJ equipment occupied the wall in between. Nothing in the way of posters, unlike Kelly's own room, which was plastered with art prints from the college store, pictures ripped from magazines and arranged into collages, and movie posters that Kelly had chosen solely for the images involved, and not because the movie in question held any importance for her.

There were no athletic trophies in Jasper's room, either, although he had accumulated a collection of them from elementary school through high school. When Kelly was a little kid, she had taken great pride in coming up behind her brother the athlete. She'd been prouder still that she could stake a similar claim to athletic talent, that this genetic gift from their father had passed on to her as well. But then Jasper quit one team sport after another, storing up all the memorabilia and hiding them in the basement. *He just wants to concentrate on track,* Kelly thought, and then when Jasper announced he'd quit track as well, she was shocked. "What will Dad think?" Kelly asked him. Jasper had given her a look. "He's a grown man, Kel. He can deal with it."

Now Kelly no longer played sports, either, but in contrast to her brother's decision, which had been sharp and deliberate as he turned instead to other things—to music and clubs and hanging out with DJs, to writing in his notebooks, to his long solitary wanderings with his iPod plugged into his ears—her own withdrawal had been a gradual thing, a fading out. The energy wasn't there. She no longer cared. She wasn't getting along with her teammates. Or her coaches.

She still wasn't ready to be alone yet. She went back to her parents' room on the off chance they were still up—or probably Hannah would be asleep, but Robert was a night owl, like her, so maybe they could go to the kitchen for hot chocolate and keep on talking—when she heard Robert say behind the closed door, ". . . just can't say that, because it's not true."

"Can't say what?" Hannah sounded the way she often did with Robert these days: weary and exasperated.

"That the past doesn't matter."

"Well, this time it doesn't. He's our son, Robert."

"Regardless of whether he's our son or not—"

"*You're* the one always saying how it's important not to dwell on things. How one of the worst things you can do is talk things to death. Which I don't agree with, by the way, but that's a whole other—"

"All I'm saying is you can forget the past but it's not like the past forgets you. And if it decides to follow you—or Jasper—into the present, you have to deal with it."

"Robert—"

"It's called *consequence*, Hannah."

"Really, Robbie? Thanks, Robbie. Because I had no idea. How do you spell that word, does it start with a C or a K—"

"Hannah—"

"To hell with consequence," Hannah thundered. "Consequence wants my son, it'll have to get through me first."

"And there's so much of you to get through," Robert said.

A moment of silence and then they both started laughing.

They could get dark and moody with each other and Hannah sometimes lost it completely with Robert, yelling at him in public as embarrassed onlookers looked away. But even the worst of their arguments tended to be like summer squalls: clearing up just as suddenly, the air fresher for it. Witnessing that dynamic play out again made Kelly feel more settled. More grounded. Maybe things would get normal again.

She left her parents alone.

But as she went into her own bedroom her mind flew back to a different kind of memory: Jasper in junior high, about to compete in a track meet somewhere in Lakefield

County. Robert was out in the driveway, doors slamming, the next-door dog barking, Robert yelling, "Jasper! Get your ass in gear! Time is money!"

And Kelly hadn't been paying attention to any of it until she opened the bathroom door and walked in on her brother. He was throwing up in the toilet. He flushed, ran a hand across his mouth. "Hey, Kel," he said casually. He went to the sink and washed his hands. He hunted through the cluttered medicine cabinet for mouthwash.

"Are you sick?" she asked him.

He shook his head. "Just nerves," he said.

"But if you're sick—"

"Look, it happens every time, okay? It's nothing." He gargled mouthwash, spat, then gargled again for good measure. "Look, whatever you do? Don't tell Dad."

"I won't."

"Don't tell Dad or I'll find your diary and make copies and post it all around the school. Hell, all around the town."

"Don't be a psycho. I said I wouldn't. And I don't keep a diary."

"Yes, you do," he said, and she wondered how he knew that.

She saw his muscles go tight along his jawline and a flat, dead look stole through his eyes. It was what their father called Jasper's game face, but it made Kelly uneasy. She was just as competitive as Jasper was—maybe more so, at least in some things—but knew intuitively that whatever game face she developed as she grew older, it would not look like her brother's.

As she followed him into the hall, she said, "Good luck. I bet you set a record."

"It doesn't matter," he said, and his voice seemed just as dead as his eyes: game voice to match the game face. "It's bullshit."

And then he was out of the house, strolling toward their father in the driveway. Through the open window, Kelly could hear their banter and laughter, hear Robert clapping his hands together, saying, "Time to do some damage." Jasper was nodding and smiling absently as if the boy she'd encountered in the bathroom—*happens all the time, don't tell Dad*—didn't exist. Except, as he caught eyes with her through the kitchen window—in that half second before he made a face and waved good-bye—they both knew he did. That it would be one of the secrets between them.

Now, she went into her own room but felt too keyed up to sleep. She could fix herself a secret gin and tonic, except after the events of tonight it just seemed wrong. Moments later, Kelly was parked on the couch in the den, flipping through late-night TV. *Notorious* was playing on one of the movie channels. It was in black and white, but the heroine was pretty cool, and not in some lightweight, "spunky," girl-next-door kind of way.

Her eyes finally closed and she drifted off.

"Have a piece," said the pale-haired man as he held out a knife and fork.

Kelly looked at the strange thing on her plate. "What is it?"
"Your brother's soul. Tasty. Like yours."
And he winked.

She woke up. Something woke her. Her father's voice. More specifically, the alarm in her father's voice, as he talked on the phone in the kitchen.

Kelly got to him just as he was hanging up. He was scowling.

"What's up?" Kelly said.

"Go back to bed, Kelly."

"I haven't really been to bed."

And now his scowl was for her. "You realize you have school in a couple of hours? You are *not* skipping."

"It's nothing ten Red Bulls can't cure," Kelly said. "What's wrong?"

But he was already stalking the hallway, grabbing his jacket from the closet. "The restaurant," he muttered and threw a word over his shoulder that sounded like *vandals*.

"Somebody trashed the place?"

"Assholes on motorcycles," Robert said.

Kelly said immediately, "I want to come with you."

"Kelly." He was in the doorway now, turning to face her. He jabbed a finger in the air. "*School.*" And then he was gone, the car backing down the driveway.

*   *   *

The restaurant was in the heart of downtown Selridge. The big chain stores along the highway had sucked business away from the downtown merchants and the city was responding with renovations: old-fashioned iron lampposts and benches, mosaic-tiled sidewalks, and strategically placed saplings were starting to give the neighborhood a quaint and intimate feel. But Kelly thought it felt fake, like a theme park, designed more for tourists than the actual people who lived here.

She chained her bike to a guardrail. Her father was standing on the sidewalk talking to a police officer. The sign to his restaurant, Spirits, hung above a smashed wall of window. Broken glass lay scattered like puzzle pieces along the window frame and hardwood floor inside.

Her father glanced over, did a slight double take. "School," he said, "is that way." He pointed.

"I'll get there. I've got time."

Kelly peered through the window. The dining room was done in taupe and a dusty olive green, with a sunken room in back that held the bar and stone fireplace. When she was a little kid, Kelly thought this place was the height of sophistication and chic.

". . . high number of complaints the last few days," the police officer was saying. "You know that old Heath house up in the hills?"

"Of course."

"Someone finally bought it, seems to be using it as some kind of clubhouse."

Kelly broke in. "A clubhouse? Like, a motorcycle gang?"

The officer looked at her. "You must be the daughter."

Kelly said, "There were these guys on motorbikes bothering us the other night? At the Diamond Dog?"

"What do you mean, they were bothering you?"

"They were just—they were bothering everybody, not just us." Although Kelly suddenly thought this might not be true. In fact, she knew it wasn't.

"Did they say anything to you?"

"Not really."

"Not really?"

"One of them said something about 'the sister,' that's all." But she felt very uncomfortable now, as if she might be betraying Jasper in some way. Except surely she wasn't. Those guys were a menace, they didn't have anything to do with him. Right? Maybe she should just shut up? Yet she couldn't seem to. "'Is that the sister.'"

"Were they referring to you?"

"I don't know."

"Were they looking at you when they said it?"

As she looked from one man to the other, she felt a shadow move through her. She saw something in her father's face that made her say, "This *does* have something to do with Jasper, doesn't it? Dad," she said, as Robert sighed and looked away from her, spreading his fingers across his jaw. "Dad, please, you have to tell me."

Robert muttered something beneath his breath that sounded like, "The bar."

More smashed glass: scattered across the dark wood floor, gleaming on the empty tables, splintering beneath her sneakers. The shelves above the bar were in ruins and the air reeked of alcohol. Cracks webbed out along the wall and in some places the mirror had broken off to show the shiny black backing beneath. Splashed across in neon spray paint were the words:

JASPER COME BACK TO US
COME BACK COME BACK COME BACK

CHAPTER SIX

Word spread fast.

As soon as she pushed through the high school doors, Ashley Powell and Gina Shapiro and Taryn Hill were springing off the lobby benches, swarming round her, demanding, "Is it true? Is he back? Did he really come back?"

Other kids joined them, their words overlapping. Kelly stopped, squeezing the strap of her knapsack, picking through the layers of voices and words to ascertain that someone's older brother and his friend had witnessed a guy who looked amazingly like Jasper Ruland emerge from the bus terminal last night and Taryn herself claimed to have sighted him walking along King Road, had rolled down her car window as she passed and yelled an experimental "Jasper?" and Jasper had reacted to the sound of his name, turning his head, but then stared coolly at Taryn as if he'd never seen her before. "But that was him," Taryn said, "wasn't it?"

Kelly confirmed that it was. She tucked her head as if bracing against a strong wind and made her way through the halls toward her locker. Kids followed, some of them falling away only to be replaced by others, who had also caught wind of Jasper's return or were simply curious to see what the fuss was about. Questions piled like crashed cars on a freeway. Kelly didn't, couldn't answer them. She was still seeing the damage to her father's beloved restaurant, the words splashed so violently across the broken mirrored wall. Her hands were shaking as she dialed the combination to her lock. Too much caffeine. Not enough sleep. She was tired and wired at the same time and felt like she might be sick. Kids talked to her and at her and, when she ignored them, to each other, as if it didn't even matter whether or not she was there.

". . . Dan Santas says he saw him walking up Pollack Avenue—"

"Santas is a pathological liar—"

"—which doesn't necessarily *mean* he was lying—"

Madison Cavillari, whom Kelly had never liked, even when they were hanging out at the mall together, pushed through the crowd and got right in Kelly's face. Madison had never liked her much, either, and now felt no need to hide it. "So is he going to own up to killing two people?"

Kelly slammed shut the locker door. Walked away. Madison fell into step beside her. The others trailed like ducklings. "That accident wasn't his fault." She'd said this so many times before, it was like she didn't even have to be present in this conversation; all she had to do was press play and step out of herself and watch the dialogue unfold.

"He was driving," Madison said.

"That was never proven."

"It was never not proven."

"You can't *not prove* that purple unicorns exist," Kelly said crossly. "That doesn't mean it's *likely*."

"No one's talking about purple unicorns."

"You were there at the accident, you know he was driving?"

"He was high."

"He doesn't touch that stuff." Guilt stroked her, a finger on her spine. Maybe it should have been her in that accident, not her brother. *He always plays it so straight.*

"He was coming back from a rave—" Madison said.

"Yeah, it was a concert, not some crazy druggy orgy, Madison, no matter what your mommy and daddy might have told you."

"Just seems like an innocent man would have stuck around." Madison smiled and brushed her styled, angled bangs from her eyes. "Especially a man with Harvard on the line."

The last was like a needle going into Kelly's skin. Innocent people stuck around, stuck up for themselves, partly because they couldn't believe they were suspects in the first place. They figured that at some point the madness would clear, people would return to their senses, justice and truth would prevail. Unless they had some compelling reason to believe otherwise. Did Jasper have such a reason?

The buzzer went off. The hallway cleared with miraculous speed. Doors swung shut up and down the hall. Madison was still staring at Kelly, her glossy lips arranged in a smirk.

"Harvard's overrated," Kelly said and pushed past her into the classroom.

She darted from first to second period without too much trauma, but another crowd formed around her just before lunch. By now, kids were also asking about the vandalism to her father's restaurant, if Jasper's name had really been written on the glass in blood ("No," she snorted, yet felt an inward chill, because even though it wasn't true, it somehow felt and seemed true), was it gang-related, was it drugs, was it some crazy psycho stalker? "Some biker chick," said Andy Stahl, the student president, and sniggered.

"Enough!" Amy descended upon the scene, hands out like a traffic cop. She pushed her way through to Kelly and slung an arm across her shoulders in a gesture both protective and territorial. "This girl is going through some major drama, all right? Some big-time heavy shit. So back the hell up. Let the girl breathe." She waved her free hand imperiously. "Vanish. Now."

"Later, Kelly," someone said and the throng reluctantly dissolved.

Kelly banged shut her locker door.

Amy said quickly, "Look, I heard. I know. I won't ask anything. You can tell me when you're ready."

"Okay," Kelly said.

"Just, soon. Please be ready soon."

"I'm late," Kelly said, although she wasn't late for anything and Amy knew it.

"Okay," Amy said, trying not to look hurt. "I've got drama club anyway. I'll see you around."

She was sitting underneath the football bleachers, plugged into her iPod, when a shadow slipped across the dirt and scrubby grass. She looked up, squinting against the glare of sun, and smiled. She dropped the earphones into her hand.

"And this is where she goes when she wants to be alone," Nick said.

He crouched in front of her, in the damp, shadowed space beneath the bleachers, clasping his hands between his knees. His face was tanned more than usual, his short hair tousled from his habit of rubbing his hand through it. Beyond, Kelly could hear the shouts and whistle blowing of soccer practice. It sounded faint, like it was happening a world away. "Don't ask me any questions about Jasper," she said. "Swear to God, I can't take it anymore."

"I was going to ask you something else—"

"You have an earring," she said suddenly. There was a small glittering rock in Nick's right earlobe. "A diamond?"

"Just a little one."

"Nick, you've got a freaking diamond in your ear."

Nick touched it self-consciously. "My grandma died—"

"She died last night?"

"No . . ." He shrugged, looked self-conscious. "Before the divorce. She left my mother these earrings, and my mother just decided that we should share them. So she had one made into a necklace for herself and the other one is for me."

"She put that thing in your ear?"

"She literally put this thing in my ear. She said I needed some kind of coming-of-age ritual, you know, like when tribes send boys out to kill lions or have visions or whatever. And come back a man. Because I'm man of the house now, you know?"

Kelly folded and then unfolded her legs as she worked this out. "Putting a diamond in your ear makes you a man."

"No. Putting a diamond in my ear will piss off my dad. Plus she thinks it's cool. But the coming-of-age talk makes her feel all smart and spiritual."

"I bet she hangs those dreamcatcher things," Kelly said.

"She does, actually." He rubbed his nose. He had a light scattering of freckles along his nose that Kelly hadn't noticed before. Seemed these days she was always noticing new things about Nick. "Do I look like a dumb-ass or should I keep it?"

"Keep it. Are you sure your mother's sane?"

"She prefers the term *eccentric*. You know. Like Howard Hughes."

"Howard Hughes was out of his freaking mind."

"I needed to find and tell you. Someone trashed our memorial."

"What?"

"Jamie Fisher skipped homeroom to go down there with some roses—it's Kira's birthday today, did you know?—and a poem she wrote for Kira and she said the place was completely—" Nick looked away from her, pulling at the back of his neck. "Trashed."

"Trashed. Vandalized," Kelly said.

"Yeah."

"Were there any words?"

His gaze jerked back to her. "What?"

"Was there anything, you know, *written* somewhere?"

"You mean like at the restaurant. I don't know. Jamie never said and it didn't occur to me to ask—"

"I need to see it," Kelly said. She stood up, brushing the dirt from her jeans, collecting her red nylon knapsack. "Let's go."

"You mean now?"

"You have Truck, right?"

She moved her shoulder just so and gave him a look of appeal. It was the kind of look she'd copied from movies and TV and practiced in mirrors. This was the first time she'd tried it on an actual human. Judging from Nick's expression, it seemed to be having an effect.

He made a token effort at resistance. "I have AP history in ten, is what I have."

"Well." Should she shake back her hair or would that be overkill? Instead she just grinned. "You don't mind missing *that*."

"I don't? . . . oh, good."

Nick loved his truck. It was one of the first things Kelly

had learned about him. There wasn't a lot of personal stuff Nick seemed to feel comfortable talking about, at least not when you first met him, but he could go on and on about his truck. He'd spent the last two summers painting houses and now worked part-time for his uncle, a general contractor. He'd put almost all of the money into this dented Chevy that now lurched and bounced its way past the edge of town. Once Kelly had asked him, "You ever think of giving it a name?"

"Sure," Nick said, patting the dashboard. "I call it Truck."

"Simple," Kelly said.

"Yet effective. And easy to remember."

He'd been joking, except Kelly would catch herself thinking of the truck in exactly that way—like a third member of their little group. Kelly and Nick and Truck, partners in crime. As Truck crested another hill, Kelly looked out into the valley and heard herself say, as if from far away, "That's where the rave was."

The valley belonged to a rancher who had agreed to lease the property for a moonlight rave, a legal event that had been four months in the making. Jasper knew the promoter and had volunteered to help pull the whole thing together. For weeks Kelly had listened to Jasper complain about the hassle of permits and enthuse about the DJs who had agreed to take turns spinning that night; she had never seen her brother look or sound so . . . starstruck. Kelly once again marveled at the bitter irony of it. Jasper had headed out to that event expecting the best night of his life; it had resulted in the death of his friends and his own self-imposed exile.

"I still can't understand why I don't remember more," Kelly said. "Why so much of that night is just a blank for me."

"Like I keep telling you," Nick said. "It was a long time ago. Why should you expect to remember the details?"

"It's not the details. It's everything . . ." They'd had this conversation before, but every now and then Kelly felt the need to have it again, as if by talking enough she'd finally get answers. "I remember how much I wanted to go—and how pissed I was because I was grounded—but then there's, well, nothing. I remember being in the hospital, I remember the nurse telling us that Jasper had just—had disappeared. I remember searching for him and talking to the police about him. But that was the next day. So that's, like, one whole entire night gone from my memory."

"It was a traumatic night," Nick said reasonably. "Trauma does that, you know. You block out stuff that's too painful to remember."

"But nothing happened to me because I wasn't even there. So shouldn't it work the other way around? I mean, you remember where you were on 9/11, right? When you found out what happened? You remember stuff about that day, don't you? Details?"

Nick winced. "Yeah," he said uncomfortably. "But that—"

"So do I," Kelly said. "But I don't remember where I was or how I found out about Jasper's accident. I mean, it must have been at home. It must have been early in the morning. Maybe police came to the door or something. But that's the point. I don't remember."

"Ask your mom and dad," Nick said.

Kelly blinked. "I don't know why I never thought of doing that," she said. But that wasn't true. It was as if that night was a festering wound in her memory and her mind recoiled from going too near it. "Besides, we don't talk about the stuff that really hurts. Did you?"

"Did I what?"

"Go to the rave?"

"No." But he looked at her when he said it and Kelly saw a shadow pass behind his eyes. "I don't even like that type of music. You know that. You know I didn't go."

Nick parked Truck and they got out, doors slamming. Starlings exploded up from the bushes. They walked a little deeper into the woods, the trees vaulting above them. The air filled with a soft, rustling hush.

Twigs snapped beneath her boots and she pushed a tangle of skinny branches out of her face.

The memorial was still upright, but had been smashed in and broken so that now the obelisk was deformed, twisting in on itself. Splintery pieces of wood were scattered in the dirt amid moss and dried leaves. Word had gotten around about the memorial and flowers and photographs had appeared at its base. Now the flowers were crushed, ripped up, scattered. The air smelled faintly of roses. There were tire tracks in the mud. Tracks of motorcycles.

"It was them," Kelly said.

"The same guys who trashed your dad's restaurant?"

"Yeah."

"How do you know?"

She pointed. Spray-painted across two trees growing near each other were the words: MY SOUL TO TAKE.

There was no sound except the wind whispering in the leaves, knocking the tree limbs together. Kelly shivered. The air felt colder.

Nick said, "Kind of an out-of-the-way place for some random destruction—"

"It wasn't random," Kelly said. She picked up a piece of wood that was sharp at the end, like a stake. A fragment of an eye was painted along the side. She would keep this piece, she decided, as a souvenir. She slipped it in her knapsack. Her heart ached for their ruined project but there were other things weighing on her. She looked at Nick. "They're sending messages to my brother."

"What?"

"They want my brother," Kelly said. "I don't know why."

Of course you don't.

She jumped. The voice, a man's voice, had whispered right in her ear.

He lies to you.

But there was no one here except for her and Nick, and Nick was too far away. In any case, this voice was too smooth, too silky . . .

He's been lying to you all this while.

Nick said, "Kelly? What's wrong?"

"Do you hear that?"

I could tell you the truth, little girl. The truth that lurks underneath and in-between things. All you have to do is come to me.

"Kelly? Are you—"

"I'm fine." She was scanning the trees. For the briefest of moments she thought she saw a tall pale-haired figure slipping behind an old oak—but she didn't see it again, and heard no sounds of movement, no rustling of leaves or snapping of branches.

The voice rubbed up against her ear: *Go ahead, ask him. Ask him about me, see how he evades and denies. You can't trust him, sweetheart. You never could.*

Darkness rushed at her. The trees tilted away at strange angles and the whole world went silent. She realized she was on the ground. Nick was bending over her, moving his mouth but she heard nothing, no voice, no sound, deep quiet and darkness pushing in around her. She was back inside the coffin, falling away from the world, but this time she wasn't alone. There was another presence in there with her. *Ask your brother about me,* the silky voice said again. *Go ahead, see what happens.*

And then Nick's voice burst through to her: "Kelly," and she was rolling over onto her knees, pressing her hands against her mouth.

I am going so very, very crazy, she thought frantically, but aloud she said, "Did you hear that? That voice? Do you hear it?"

"No."

"So then I'm crazy? Is that it?" She was on her feet, pulling away from him. She picked her way up the slope, to-

ward the thicket of trees where she'd caught that glimpse of
blonde hair. Her hand tightened on the wooden stake in her
hand—it made her feel better to have some kind of weapon,
no matter how pathetic.

I only want what's already mine . . .

"Wait." Nick said, surprising her. "Wait. Yeah. I heard
that."

"You did? I'm not crazy? There's somebody out there?"

He was looking around.

"You're right, you're not crazy, and we should get the hell
out of here."

Aren't you going to ask me who I am?

"Let's go, Kelly," Nick said, in a stern voice of reason that
made him sound like someone's father.

Don't you want to know my name?

Kelly yelled into the woods, "Why should I care?"

Something rustled in the undergrowth . . . but it was
only a squirrel, springing up into an elm, its small dark body
disappearing through leaves. But emerging from behind the
tree was something else. Someone else. A tall slender figure, standing motionless in profile except for the pale hair
blowing back from his forehead. Kelly didn't realize she had
stepped back until she felt herself jostle Nick, who took her
hand and whispered something in her ear that she didn't
make out. She was staring too intently at this man. This
man who had some kind of business—bad business—with
her brother.

"You know my name," the man whispered. "You know it."

Whispered, yet somehow she could hear him perfectly,

despite the wind in the trees and the distance between them and the thump of her pulse in her ears.

She summoned defiance. She was her father's daughter, tough and feisty, not some wilting princess easily intimidated. "Why should I care?"

She saw his grin, which seemed very big and white in profile, eating up the lower half of his face. "Ask your brother," he said.

Wind kicked up, swirling his coat around his legs, and it started to rain. Kelly looked up at the first strokes of wet on her face and when she looked in the direction of the man, he was gone. "I've seen him before," she said. She felt herself surging forward, ready to give chase, track down this mystery, but Nick was hauling her back toward Truck.

"Are you *insane*?" he said. "We came. We saw. We go *home*. Get it?"

She got it.

CHAPTER SEVEN

Prodigal Son: . . . a son who returns home after losing his fortunes. The term is now widely used regarding a son who does not live up to the expectations of those who have launched him (or perhaps her) into life or career. The phrase "prodigal son" might also refer to the change of direction in someone's life, when he leaves home or when he returns home.

Kelly sat back in her chair and reread the lines on the computer screen. She had been taking fresh towels to the bathroom off Jasper's bedroom when she ducked into the study to check the meaning of the phrase. Her father had said it with affection and delight, yet it didn't exactly sound like a compliment.

A change in the direction of someone's life.

That seemed true enough, and maybe that's what her father had meant. Jasper had come home in order to change the direction of his life. That seemed okay.

She picked up the lemon-scented towels and walked down the hallway, sock feet sinking into carpet. The door to her parents' bedroom was closed. Behind it she could hear her mother talking on the phone: ". . . insist on getting him in for a physical, who knows how long it's been and he looks malnourished and underweight, drained of every ounce of energy—"

The door to Jasper's room was slightly open. She knocked and heard him say, "Come in."

"Towels for you," Kelly said.

He buried his face in the topmost one, took a deep appreciative whiff. "Fresh clean towels. Beautiful."

Kelly said, "So what did you do all day?"

"Slept. Watched TV. Called a guy about a job."

"Did you get it?"

"Yeah, the manager at Falstaff's knows me from when I was working for Dad and still likes me. Even though . . . you know. I start Monday. Split shifts, which I'm not crazy about, and probably not a whole lot of hours at first. But it's a start."

"Dad would have hired you."

"I don't need to be working for Dad. Been there, done that."

"I could never do the front-of-the-house stuff," Kelly said.

"You'd be a good hostess."

"I'd rather be on the line. But Dad doesn't want me in the kitchen. Says it's too rough and macho for a tender young thing like myself."

Jasper yawned. "That's 'cause there's a lot of profanity and harassment and cocaine. No, that's probably not true. Forget I said that."

"You're tired," Kelly observed.

Jasper rubbed his eyes. "I'm fine. I'm fine." Something defensive in his voice. Something worried. Kelly recalled what she'd overheard her mother say about getting him in for a physical. She was going to remark on that—on how he should look after himself, take good care of himself, now that he was back for a fresh start and a change in direction, even if she didn't think her father was right in pegging him as a *prodigal son*. But what came out of her mouth was something else entirely.

"I know you're in trouble," she said.

He took a step back as the breeze swept through the window and moved the faded blue curtains. And she saw something—a shadow of something—pass across his face, turning his eyes careful and hooded. She knew she should have just shut up, said good night, and left, but instead she blurted, "I want to help you. I know that something really weird is going on—I know you're connected with it in some way—I don't care. I just want to help you. I want you to stay. I'm afraid you'll go away again."

She waited for him to say something.

Anything.

She said, feeling lame, "I just wanted you to know that."

He bowed his head for a moment, as if working through a line of thought. For a moment she thought—hoped—that he would say, "What are you talking about, Kel, you sound like a damn fool," and she would shake her head and feel stupid, sure, but also very, very relieved. "I'm home now," she wanted him to say, "and that's the important thing. Everything is going to be fine from here on out. Everything's going to be great."

But what he actually said was, "I appreciate that, little sister, but there are some things that just don't concern you, things you shouldn't have anything to do with," and next thing she knew he was gently but firmly pushing her into the hallway and closing the door in her face.

"Hey," she said. She tried the door but it was locked. She kicked it. Kicked it again. "Hey. You can't do that to me! You hear me?" She waited. "I know you hear me, you jerk. *So* immature." When he didn't reply, she kicked the door again and said, "I'm not going anywhere. I'll just stay here and yell and annoy you so much you'll jump out the window and *die*."

He opened the door so swiftly she had to take a step back.

"Look," he said, "I'm sorry. I shouldn't have done that."

"I love this new habit you have of apologizing," she said. "You never used to do that at all." She stepped into the room and shut the door behind her and turned to face him with her hands on her hips. "Talk to me."

He was looking at her and shaking his head. "You're a piece of work," he said. "Were you always like this?"

"Yes. You just didn't notice. Because you're oblivious."

"No. I always noticed you, even when I pretended otherwise. You would never let me *not* notice." He lifted his hands a little, then let them fall. "It's complicated."

"Complicated?" she said. "You want to know what's complicated?"

"Okay, Kel, I can guess where you're going with this and—"

"Complicated is when your brother disappears and you have no idea why. Not even a phone call that explained anything. Not even a note. How could you do that to us? To *Mom*? It's like a grenade went off, you know, and we've been wandering around the aftermath for months."

"I'm back now."

"Not even an e-mail."

"It's not like I had regular access to the Internet."

"There are Internet cafés all over the place. Not even a postcard. You didn't have access to postcards, either?"

"I'm back now," Jasper said.

"Yeah? For how long?"

"I messed up. I know that. I seriously screwed up this family and I am so sorry, Kelly."

"Apologizing again," she said.

"Yeah, well, it's sincere. You have to believe me on that."

"You know, apologizing isn't enough. It really isn't."

He gave a slight nod.

"But it's a start," she allowed.

"I'm not going anywhere."

"Not even to Harvard?"

"Oh, Harvard." He rolled his eyes.

"Mom and Dad will want you to—"

"Since when are you so concerned about what Mom and Dad want? How's your own life going, Kel? What about your own plans for the Great Beyond?"

"The what?"

Was she really going to let herself get sidetracked like this? Apparently so.

"Life after high school. You think high school will never end, but all of a sudden it does. And you're staring at the rest of your life. And you realize that school was this teeny-tiny part of it." He held his thumb and forefinger about an inch apart.

"Says the guy who hasn't managed to graduate yet."

He shrugged. "Just a few courses. It'll be easy."

"I haven't . . ." She paused. "I've been preoccupied," she said. "I mean, the future happens anyway, right? You should live in the moment."

"True. Except the moment has a way of turning into the next moment. So if all you do is live in the moment, you might find yourself trapped in a really crappy moment. Where will you be in the next moment, Kel?"

"Why are we talking about me?" she said irritably. "You totally changed the subject. We were talking about you."

"Until you went off on me. Besides, I want to know how you are."

"I'm . . ." She flung up her hands. "I'm not as smart any-more, okay? My grades aren't so great anymore, okay?"

"Are they bad?"

"No. Because then Mom and Dad would never let me out of the house—"

"Ah." He nodded in understanding.

"Keep in mind it's not like they're paying a whole lot of attention."

"They are. They might not seem like it, but they are."

"All their attention," Kelly said, "went to you. Always. That's just the way it's always been."

She expected him to deny, to say, "You're imagining things," but instead he shrugged and said, "Yeah, well. Would have been better for both of us if that wasn't the case." Then he looked at her sharply, as if just now hearing what she had said moments ago. "What do you mean you're not as smart? You're just as smart now as you've ever been."

"You made me smarter," she mumbled.

"That's really screwed-up logic, Kel."

"Because you were always so brilliant." The words came with more force than she'd expected. "And I had to follow you up through the grades—I always had the same teachers you had, and the teachers always remembered you—"

Jasper gave a nod. "The burden of expectations."

"That's the thing! There was no burden. Not for me. . . . Mom and Dad were constantly telling you how important it was to live up to your gifts, your potential. But nobody seemed to care much about my potential. So if a C was good enough for me, then why try any harder? Why fight the double standard? That's how it seemed to me."

"You got that all wrong," Jasper said. "Mom and Dad just wanted to make sure you didn't feel lost in my shadow."

"Condescending to me wasn't the way to do it."

"I never knew you felt like this."

"We'd be at the dinner table and Dad would be talking about how well you did at the science fair, and then there'd be this guilty silence, and Mom and Dad would look at me, and Dad would say, 'And you, Kelly, look at you, you're using your left hand just as well as your right!' I mean, even a kid can recognize that as—"

"I think it would be cool to be ambidextrous," Jasper said.

"Don't," Kelly said. "Don't tell me I'm being oversensitive about this stuff. Okay? My only point was—the only one who expected better, higher things from me seemed to be you. And you were the one who took me to bookstores, because Mom and Dad were always so busy, always telling me how important reading was, but I didn't know . . . I didn't know who to read, or where to start, or why reading on my own would be any better than the reading they shove down your throat at school."

"Some of those books you study at school are pretty cool," Jasper remembered. *"Lord of the Flies*—"

"I hated *Lord of the Flies,*" Kelly said. "A bunch of school-boys running around some stupid island picking on the fat kid? It's like a really demented episode of *Survivor.*"

"To Kill a Mockingbird," Jasper said.

"Okay. That's a good one. But most of the others—"

He grinned. "I remember that first trip to the bookstore.

You bought, like, *Sweet Valley High* and *The Baby-Sitters Club*."

"Last spring I read *Crime and Punishment*," she said.

"You're reading Dostoyevsky on your own but your GPA is a—"

"Let us not talk of the GPA," she said darkly. "You made me smart. That's the way I always saw it. So when you went away, it's like I went dumb again."

"Kelly, that makes no sense whatsoever."

"It's not about logic! It's about—you know—it's psychological stuff!" She picked at her cuticles.

"It's easy to fall," he said. "We all fall apart sometimes. There's no shame in it. The trick is what you do next."

Fall. Kelly wanted to object to the word. It's not like she'd fallen all that far—okay, Harvard was out of the question for her, but it had never been in the question. That was Jasper's deal, Jasper's brilliance. She was meant for other things. She'd accepted that. But she thought of that last night dropping ecstasy with Amy and Morgan—how reckless and powerful and invulnerable she felt in such moments. It was the kind of way you wanted to feel all the time. And she was a curious girl; she felt it in her bones; she wanted to see everything, taste everything, try everything, go everywhere, including the places she wasn't supposed to. She didn't think that kind of curiosity, or sense of adventure, was a bad thing. But if you were trying to escape other things, as well—things like hurt and loneliness—if you were trying to do things just for the easy fix of feeling better . . . It was as if a window opened and Kelly caught a flash of a road she was on, which didn't seem so bad now but would keep taking her to darker places.

But then the window closed just as suddenly as it had opened and she was damn sick of thinking and talking about this. "What about you," she said. She remembered what her father had said the other night behind the closed bedroom door. "What about the consequences?"

He looked at her.

"What about Dad's restaurant getting trashed?" she said. "What about the stuff they wrote? They trashed my memorial, too, did you know? They're hanging out at the old Heath place."

"They'll be gone soon. They can't stay in one place for long."

"Why not?"

"They just can't. Trust me on this."

"What if you're wrong?"

"I'm not going to let anything bad happen to you." His eyes were a vivid blue, the same color as her own, an unusual and dominant gene passed down from their father. Looking into her brother's eyes was a bit like looking into the mirror. She wondered if her brother ever felt the same, or if it was just some sick expression of narcissism on her part. "It's hard for me to put this kind of stuff into words. But you can trust me. You need to trust me."

He was being evasive, which annoyed her. He also seemed world-weary in a way that unnerved her, so she decided it wasn't real, it was just a pose, but this annoyed

her also. She used the name like a weapon, not to hurt
him but to shock, maybe enough to get some kind of answer:

"Who's Archie?"

And he jerked away from her, as if the name was a fire-
cracker exploding between them.

He stood up and paced to the wall. When he turned to
face her again, his face was a blank, careful mask. He said,
"Where did you get that name?"

"Does it matter?"

Truth was, she wasn't quite sure. The man in the woods
was the same man from the classroom. She had no doubt
about that. But in the classroom he had identified himself
as Mr. Archer.

"Kelly." This tone of voice—this sheer, you-are-so-
annoying-me-right-now kind of exasperation—was familiar,
as well. "It matters. Tell me how you got that name."

"Tell me who he is. Tell me what he wants from you."

"Tell me how you got that name."

"You tell me, I tell you." What was the expression?
From that intense scary movie with the actress her mother
liked? "Quid pro quo." She waited a moment, then said
sarcastically, "Because it's hard for me to put this stuff into
words."

She thought they had reached some kind of standstill,
like they often did when they were younger, when his will
clashed with her will and no progress seemed possible.
Then his eyes flickered for a moment—just a moment—

but she knew what he'd been looking at and her hand came up to touch her face. Her scars, so faded now they were almost invisible, unless you knew where to look. Jasper always knew.

"They fade more every year," he said.

She sensed a small window opening up between them. She grabbed the chance and dove through it. "Jasper. I need to know. Who is Archie?"

"He's—" And she saw that mask of his dissolving as he spun away from her and sighed and looked up at the ceiling. "There's this kind of motorcycle cult. They call themselves the Ride. Archie's the leader."

"So it's like the Hells Angels or something? But—"

"They're not like anything you've ever read about. And neither is Archie."

"So what is he?" He didn't answer. "Jasper," she said impatiently. "I mean, he's got to be human, right? At the very least?" He still wouldn't answer.

And then the realization came to her, moved through her like a cold wind. "He's not human," Kelly said flatly. "He's not human. You are not really telling me this."

"This isn't *telling*." Correcting her even now. "It's more like *implying*."

"You are not really *implying* this."

She had never seen her brother's eyes look so bleak.

Jasper took a breath, said, "He's some kind of fallen—" when movement from the doorway caught their attention.

Their mother was leaning against the doorframe. Her face was very pale. She had pulled on a coat and the cowboy boots their uncle had brought her from Texas. She said, "Jasper, you need to drive me to the hospital. Something's wrong. I'm bleeding."

CHAPTER EIGHT

"Placenta previa," the doctor explained a few hours later. "It's when the placenta implants too low in the womb, too close to the opening of the cervix." Kelly nodded. She knew this from before; it was the reason why her mother was on bed rest in the first place.

But Jasper was still figuring this out. "So Mom moved around too much, and the placenta ripped, and that's what caused the bleeding?"

Hannah had been laid out on the curtained-off hospital bed and the nurse had searched for the babies' two heart-beats, spreading gel across her mother's belly and moving the little white probe across the skin. The first heartbeat was easy to find, strong and fast like a jackhammer. The nurse taped the probe over the baby's heartbeat and a green line settled into a steady jagged rhythm on the monitor above her mother's head. That was Baby A. The nurse picked up the second probe and started looking for Baby B. Kelly could see her mother fighting for calm, hands clenching at her sides, until she cried out, "Oh my God, where's the heartbeat?"

"Easy," Robert said quietly, touching her shoulder.

"Here he is," the nurse said. "He's just tucked himself way down here, that's all. Sometimes the little rascals aren't that easy to find."

Kelly looked at the monitor as Baby B's heartline jumped to life beneath Baby A's. She looked to her mother. They had set up an IV line running into her mother's wrist and were preparing to move her to a room.

"The problem now is that the bleeding has irritated the uterus, and so she's having minor contractions," the doctor said.

Kelly said, "She's going into premature labor?"

"Not if we can help it. We're going to give her some medicine to stop them. We don't want the babies to be born yet."

Kelly said, "And if they do get born? Would they survive?"

"There's a good chance they'd survive."

"But would they be okay? Healthy?"

"Kelly," her father said in a voice that had turned very soft, "why don't you go downstairs to the newsstand and buy your mother some magazines?"

Later, when Hannah had been moved to a single room on the fifth floor, Kelly managed a minute alone with her while

Robert and Jasper went to the cafeteria. Hannah pushed hair off her face. She looked flushed. "It's the medicine," she said, gesturing to the IV pole. "This stuff makes my heart beat faster."

"But you're okay?"

"Just very big and uncomfortable and tired right down through my bones."

"And the babies?" Kelly said. "They'll be okay?"

"Do you want to feel them?"

Kelly scraped her chair closer to the hospital bed and placed a hand on her mother's belly. She was surprised all over again at how taut it felt. She felt a hard flick against her palm and the surface of her mother's stomach dove and rippled, as if one of the babies had ducked for cover. Kelly laughed. "That's so great."

"Isn't it?" Her mother's eyes were bright. "Isn't it amazing? These babies are going to turn our lives inside out and sometimes I'm not sure how we'll cope, but—isn't it the most amazing thing?"

"I want to be a good big sister."

She hadn't realized this until now. Outside of her own complicated feelings for Jasper, she'd never thought much about the sibling thing at all. You didn't always get along with your brothers or sisters and half the time you didn't have much in common. You'd much rather be with your friends. But even your closest of friends never had the exact same eye color as you. And no matter how closely you confided the stuff of your family history, that was never the same as sharing life inside it, seeing the world filtered through it.

Because the things you did have in common with your sibling were things you'd never have in common with anybody else. It felt like a big realization unfolding inside her and so obvious that she wondered why she'd never thought it before.

"You will, honey. You'll look out for them the way Jasper looks out for you."

"Jasper tore the heads off my dolls."

"The twins probably won't have dolls."

"Jasper," Kelly said. "Mom, there's something about Jasper—"

"Yes," her mother murmured, "you need to tell me about Jasper . . ."

But her eyes were closing and a moment later she was asleep.

Their father would spend the night in Hannah's room. Only one visitor was allowed to do so. "Go home," he told Kelly and Jasper. "Get some sleep. Come back tomorrow."

"But we can sleep on the couches in the waiting room," Kelly said. "I don't see why we have to—"

"You two need to take care of yourselves," their father said. "Get some real sleep. Eat some real food. Not this vending machine or this cafeteria crap. Okay?"

"But—"

"Kelly," Jasper said in a low voice. He touched her arm. "It's a good idea."

It was beginning to drizzle as they drove home, a mist of rain so light that the moisture reminded Kelly of dust motes, glinting and swirling through the streetlights. "Mom's in good hands," Jasper said, glancing sidelong at her.

"Everything just seems so on edge lately," Kelly said. "So fragile. Like it's all going to come apart any second."

Jasper was quiet for a moment as shadow and streetlight passed over his face. The CD player wasn't working properly, and there was nothing but commercials on the radio, so Jasper switched it off. The silence in the car seemed even louder than the commercial jingles had been.

"Maybe this isn't the right thing to say," he said. "But you're right, you know. Shit. Life is fragile. Things do have a way of just flying apart. So you have to—you know. Learn to deal."

"Learn to deal," Kelly echoed. She couldn't keep the sarcasm from her voice. "Oh, great advice. Great advice. You're so wise."

"Shut your mouth," Jasper said and flashed a grin at her.

"Likewise."

Something between them seemed to ease and Kelly felt comfortable enough to ask, "So why did you come back?"

"Why do you think?"

"You missed us," Kelly said. "But weren't you missing us all along? So what—what was the, you know, the triggering thing that made you drop whatever the hell you were doing with—with those guys—" For some reason she couldn't bring herself to say Archie's name. But Jasper inclined his head just a little, as if the name had passed between them anyway. "—and come home?"

Traces of a smile flickered along Jasper's mouth. He kept his eyes on the road. "You can be pretty stupid when you're young," he muttered. "Especially when you're like us."

"Like us?"

"You and me. We grew up with everything."

"Oh please. It's not like we're rich. It's not like we're jet-setting to Europe or shopping on Rodeo Drive or—"

Jasper snorted in a way that made her fall silent.

"It's not about money, Kelly. There are billionaires' kids who have it worse than us. But you know what's out there when you leave home?"

"The rest of the whole wide world?"

"Well, that. And the void," Jasper said. "The abyss. You have to be able to look straight into it. You have to have the mental strength."

"Or else what?"

"It tricks you. It eats you alive."

She wasn't sure why he was talking like this. He didn't sound like her brother—but then, the brother she had known, or thought she had known, disappeared a long time ago. She didn't know this version of her brother nearly so well.

"So you came home because . . . because of this . . . this *abyss*? Because you're not prepared for it?"

She wanted to understand where he was going with this. She really did.

"Not me," he said.

He looked at her.

She drew back against her seat.

He swung the car into their driveway.

And for some reason, as he put the car into park and switched off the ignition and the headlights cut out, putting them into darkness, another thought came to her. "You were supposed to be at Harvard right now," she said. It felt like a strange kind of echo, as if there was another, different life running underneath and parallel to this one: the life where the car accident had never happened, Jasper's future still rolling along its gilded track. And in this other life, underneath and parallel, who would she have been? Still the popular, happy-go-lucky athlete, visiting her brother at Cambridge, bragging about him when she got home. None of these strange anxiety attacks. More friends, different friends. No visions of talking coyotes.

The void. The abyss.

"Harvard," Jasper said. "Yeah."

But there was no regret in his voice.

And it finally occurred to her that maybe Harvard had never been what he wanted after all, not truly, just like he had never really wanted to compete in sports when he was a kid, even though he'd been so good at them.

Jasper got out of the car. She stayed where she was a moment longer, still absorbing their conversation, as rain tapped lightly on the windshield and mist drifted over the driveway.

In the distance, there came the sound of motorcycles.

CHAPTER NINE

"Get inside," Jasper snapped.

He was waiting for her on the porch.

Engines purred and growled through the mist, sounding closer. Kelly felt oddly detached: not afraid so much as curious, as if this was just a movie and she wanted to know what happened next.

Jasper jerked his head toward the door and she slipped past him into the hallway. The air was cold and smelled faintly of garlic and lemon-scented furniture cleaner—this was the day the cleaning lady came to set things in order and cook them her special paprika chicken. Just being in her own house made Kelly feel reassured . . . until she heard a fresh roar of motorcycles that now sounded as if they were approaching the house from all sides. A grim, worried look slipped through Jasper's features, but then his face settled into that mask that betrayed no emotion.

"Maybe we should have stayed at the hospital," Kelly said. "Maybe we should go back—"

"They would just follow us there. Mom doesn't need this on top of everything else. Whatever happens, Kelly, you stay close to me, all right?"

"What do you think is going to happen?"

The engine sounds disappeared.

The resulting silence was deep and complete. Kelly folded her arms across her chest, hugging herself, and walked into the living room. Through the gauzy curtains that lined the windows she could see only darkness and mist.

Jasper said, "I think—"

Beams of light pierced the windows, roved across the ceilings and the walls. Kelly fell back a step, feeling her jaw drop just a little, as the beams zigzagged across the corners and passed through one another, forming a shifting, restless latticework of light. They were the single-beamed headlights of motorcycles, but how come she couldn't *hear* them anymore? An icy knot formed in her stomach.

"Jasper," she whispered, "what's happening?"

"This is just a game." His voice was cold, but she knew the coldness wasn't directed at her. Lights slipped over his face and body, carving out a cheekbone, a shoulder, a glittering eye. "They're playing games, Kelly. That's all."

"You think they're out there?" she said. "They must be out there, right? How come it's so quiet? This is *nuts*—This is *home*—" As if home, just by being home, was some kind of impenetrable fortress.

"Get away from the window," Jasper said.

Something banged against the glass and Kelly jumped back. She was too startled even to shriek. The face smashed up against the window didn't look human: the eyes were too yellow, the features pulled out and distorted, like taffy. But then a grin split across it, the crooked white teeth, and she recognized the grin—the face—a twisted version of the one she had seen in the strange room at school, the teacher who wasn't a teacher, the classroom that didn't exist.

She managed not to scream. She took another step back. "Jasper," she said, reaching out for her brother, feeling his hand close over hers. The face melted back into the mist.

Something banged into the window behind her.

She couldn't help it: she shrieked.

Jasper pulled her against him.

"Don't look," Jasper muttered in her ear. "Like I said. Games. If you stay close to me they can't touch you—"

Another bang, this time against the window in the dining room.

Another bang, this time against the front door. Kelly saw something dark and misshapen pressed against the small glass inset and averted her eyes.

"They think this kind of stuff is funny," Jasper said.

He was trying for bravado, but his voice wasn't steady.

The glass was shivering in the windowframes. "Jasper," Kelly whispered, and pointed. The glass was . . . rippling, and shifting . . . and there rose a long, sighing sound, shivering across all the windows. Kelly blinked. Blinked again. *Not happening*.

And the sheets of glass came apart from the frames,

from the top and two sides, falling over like dominoes and crashing to the floor. It was a silver wave of noise breaking through the room. Broken glass skated across the hardwood floor and came flying straight at them. Jasper grabbed Kelly and spun her around, toward the stairs, shielding her. She felt a sting in her palm and raised it to her face and stared at the splinter. A drop of blood traced a line down her palm. Wind swept into the room, damp and cold, blowing hair across Kelly's eyes.

A voice said, low and cooing, "Jasper, don't you miss us? We miss you . . ."

Another voice overlapped with the first: ". . . We came here just for you . . ."

Yet another voice, higher and thinner: "Time to come home . . ."

"Come home, come home, come home . . ."

The mist was rolling through the windows now and Kelly saw vague dark shapes moving beyond them.

"I am home," Jasper yelled out suddenly. "You hear me?"

And another, different voice hissed: "Not this place. Not anymore."

And then all the voices were on them at once, moving like wind:

Getting so tired of this, Jasper.

Yeah. This town sucks. Want to be moving.

Got to keep moving.

Let's go, let's go, let's go.

"No one's stopping you!" Jasper yelled.

You are, dude. We're waiting for you.

Waiting for you to come to your senses.

You made a deal. You know that. Archie sure as hell knows that.

Laughter.

Yeah, he really, really knows that.

You think he'd just let you go?

Just 'cause you got some marks on your body?

You think he doesn't know that game? He knows that game better than anybody.

Better than you.

Way better.

Time to get back on the road.

Someone hummed a tune. *On the road again . . .*

So is this the sister? The pretty little sister?

I'd give my soul for a sister like that.

Laughter.

Does she know what you did? Does she know—

"Get upstairs," Jasper said. "Now."

But she seemed to have lost the ability to move. She was too focused on the voices, trying to decipher what they were saying, as if they weren't speaking English but some kind of code. Then she felt Jasper's hand between her shoulder blades and fresh terror swept through her as he gave her a shove, which was enough to get her stumbling toward the staircase. She tripped on the steps, grabbing wildly at the railing, and then she was pulling herself back to her feet and it took such a long time to get to the top of the stairs, a long time. Jasper was behind her. "Kelly," he said, as she hit the hallway running and then she was in her parents' room. She had gone there without thinking. It had always seemed like the strongest, safest room.

And then she was bracing herself against the corner wall, pushing at the teakwood dresser. One of its legs bumped off the Nepalese rug and screeched against hardwood. "Why won't you help me with this?" She glanced over to see Jasper standing calmly in front of the bay window. She noticed that, up here, the glass was untouched.

His voice was flat. "Because it's pointless."

"We have to do *something*!"

She turned around just in time to see the shuttered windows swing open so hard they bounced off the outside wall. Wind stormed through the room, blasting back her hair, pulling at her face. She had to close her eyes, which made her feel panicky because she didn't know where Jasper was, what was happening to him. She cried out for her brother and the wind died down and she heard him say her name. He was off to her right. The air was still now, but she was afraid to open her eyes, of what she might find in front of her. She heard faint, whispered words as if the wind itself was speaking to her. She found herself turning her face into the breeze, into those words, but she couldn't make them out. They weren't meant for her.

She opened her eyes and looked at her brother.

He had turned his back to her. He was leaning into the open window, his arms lifted at either side, like wings, hands gripping the edges of the frame. "Jasper," she said, but he gave no indication of having heard. He seemed to have forgotten all about her. He was staring down through the mist, to the street.

And he was listening. His body seemed taut, as if the words on the wind—which of course he could hear, she realized, could hear clearly and perfectly—were like small electric shocks slipping through him, one after the other, charging every inch of blood and bone.

"Jasper," she said again.

"I made a huge mistake," he said. "I shouldn't have come back here."

She realized in that moment she was losing him. Even though he was standing right in front of her, she was losing him, and this time he might never find his way back. She reached out and touched his shoulder, as if the gesture could anchor him right here in their parents' room, and drew up behind him. Beads of sweat were slipping down his face, even though it was shivering cold. Her gaze moved across his shoulder and she saw what—who—commanded his attention down below.

The strange, slender man from the classroom; from the woods. He stood alone in the middle of the street, the mist swirling around him, and gazed calmly up at her brother. His hair seemed to cast off a light of its own; he wore faded jeans and a white shirt open at the throat. He was wearing some kind of strange backpack, the mist obscuring it so she couldn't make out the details; but then the mist furled away from him and it wasn't a backpack at all.

What she saw made her knees turn to water; she had to grab at Jasper's shoulders to stop herself from falling.

Wings.

They jutted from behind the man's shoulder blades, curved edges glinting like razors. *Fake,* she thought, *they have to be fake,* except how could anything fake look this lustrous, have such graceful height and shape, seem to have a life all their own? They shifted and flickered in a very odd way; as she watched, transfixed, she saw how parts of them seemed to . . . disappear . . . and then reappear, so that the wings themselves seemed alive, pulsing in the strange light of the mist. Then they unfurled, still pulsing, the edges of them seeming to cut into air and then disappear; she had the sudden sense that this reality was not enough to contain them, that a creature like this, whatever he was, existed in more than one dimension at the same time, that these wings were impossibly vast, more so than she could ever hope to imagine, that they unfolded in all their shimmering pulsing darkness across realities other than this one. But then the thought was gone, as if it had been given to her accidentally and then yanked away. The winged stranger in the street turned his head and suddenly she was looking right into him, they were looking into each other. She saw the face of the man she had talked to in the classroom; but at the same time she could see through those pale, pleasant features to the inner face, the hidden face, the smashed distorted thing that had been snarling at her window.

Then the creature's eyes flared at her: red diamond-shaped lights that seemed to explode from his face, lifting up toward her, and she felt herself knocked off bal-

ance. She reeled backward, felt the edge of her parents'
bed bump up against her legs as she sat down heavily on
it. She pressed her palms against her eyes. She could see
the afterimage of those twin red lights, flaring as vividly
against the screen of her closed eyelids as they had in the
street below. She cried out and doubled over. It was as if
they were burning themselves into her brain. She wanted
it to stop.

Of course it was drugs, a voice, not her own, whispered
inside her.

It was all just a dream, right? Some really wild dream.

Let's go for a walk.

Or maybe my head's just screwed up from bad E.

But these were not her thoughts. The voice was like
something hot and alien, pressing against the gray folds
of her brain as it slithered through her head, leaving these
thoughts behind like a creature shedding its skin.

"Stop, stop, stop." She squeezed her temples. "Please
stop."

*You really think I could trust some loser like you? You had
everything and you blew it. For what? To go party?*

"Get out of my head," Kelly whispered. "Get out."

All you've done is feed me one lie after another.

I hope I never see you again.

Yeah. I've done ecstasy.

He's a bad influence, I guess.

"*Get out!*" Kelly screamed, and suddenly that snake of a
voice slithering through her mind was gone. Or at least, it
seemed to be gone.

Too late she realized the rest of the world was going with it. She saw Jasper moving away from the window, coming at her with fear in his eyes, but the darkness pushed in between them and the black-coffin feeling clamped itself around her and she might have screamed. She couldn't be sure. She couldn't hear anything. She was falling into the void or the void rose to take her. Either way, she was gone.

PART TWO

Notes from the Ride (II)

These are some of the things I can't tell you. At least not yet. But I need to write them out like this, maybe as practice for that day when we do sit down together and I try to explain all this to you. . . . If that day ever comes.

The first time I ever saw him, I was young enough to listen to my gut without questioning the strange things it was telling me.

That first time, Dad was driving me home from a soccer game. I was crumpled in the backseat, grass-stained and exhausted, dirty cleats kicked off so I could curl up on the ripped leather seat and read my book, which was what I'd been wanting to do all afternoon instead of chasing some stupid ball around a field while the grown-ups yelled like madmen from the sidelines. The heat of the car made me drowsy. I was fighting it, trying to read, but my eyes kept closing—until for some reason—but it wasn't a reason so much as a feeling—I lifted my head to look out the side window.

Someone was calling me.

It was as if I was hearing one thing with my mind and another with my ears. Dad was singing along with the radio, "Love in an elevator . . ." tapping one large hand on the dashboard, sleeves rolled up so that when I looked through the space between the front seats I could see the tattoo on his forearm.

We stopped at the intersection of Farris and King, the red light staring over the crossroads like an evil eye.

I remember telling you when you were little— maybe the same age that I was that day in the car— that Farris is one of the friendly streets that takes you all the places you want to go, the video arcade and toy stores and Dad's restaurant downtown, where the waitresses always made a fuss over us and told me how handsome I'd be when I grew up and how the girls would be after me. They brought extra servings of that amazing chocolate chip bread pudding they don't make anymore.

But King Avenue is a different kind of street. It's narrow and dark and rough, it loops through the hills like a snake. I never trusted it.

And so, that day, as we waited for the traffic light to change, I looked out to where King Street rose into wooded hillside.

A tall thin man was walking out of the trees and down the road's gravelly shoulder. The man wore a long *pale coat that blew around his legs. He stopped and lifted his head as if catching a scent in the air.*

He seemed to be looking straight at me.

And I got the feeling he was saying more than my name.

"Hey, kid."

"Nice little soul you got there."

It was as if the man's face opened up and I could see through it to a dark and whistling abyss.

The traffic light went to green. I ducked my head and hunched myself as low and small as I could, keeping myself below the sightline of the window, as Dad drove through the intersection and started up the hill toward home.

Home.

Home was good. Home was safe. The man and the void he brought with him would never be able to follow me there. For some reason I always believed that.

Every now and then, down through the years, he'd show up.

I saw him at the entrance gate of the annual exhibition when I was nine, as the lights flashed along the midway and the Ferris wheel turned behind him and churned out its tinny music. I saw him reflected in store windows at the shopping mall once, following just behind me . . . except when I looked behind me, he was gone. I didn't go to the mall for months after that.

Once, in junior high, I saw him standing at the end of a hall-way just as the bell rang for third period. There were all these other kids around, but it was like everybody disappeared except for him; he stared me down across the length of hall and lifted a finger and pointed at me. And I ducked into the nearest class-room and shut the door, felt my heart kicking at my ribs. Hated myself for being such a coward.

He was at Aunt Edna's funeral, at the burial service, stand-ing back amid the headstones. You asked me why I looked so pale and I had no way to answer you. So I ignored you instead and charged into the cemetery looking for him. I was fifteen and pissed off for all sorts of reasons that seemed like decent reasons at the time and I remember how the wind was blowing in my face.

He didn't want anything from me, not yet.

"In time," he told me. "In time."

"Because I've got nothing but."

CHAPTER TEN

Kelly.

She was drifting in a world of white.

Kelly. Sweet child. Over here, yes?

She turned and saw the coyote, sitting straight and prim with his tail curved neatly around his paws. He tilted his head in greeting.

"Is this a dream?" she said.

Yes. And you must wake up.

She yawned. "Fifteen more minutes. Maybe twenty. It's nice to have a break from all the— It's getting *scary* out there."

He's in your head, Kelly. Wake up now, or he'll rework your mind even more than he already has.

"Who are you?" she said. "Some kind of trickster?"

The coyote touched his nose with his paw, then gave a delicate scratch behind his ear. *You people so love to call us that,* he said.

"Who are you trying to trick?"

Not you.

"But if you're a trickster, how can I believe anything you're telling me?"

I will tell you this. He ducked his head again. *Your brother helped me once.*

"He did? How?"

You must wake up now. Yes, it may be frightening, but that is no reason to stay sleeping.

"How did he help you?"

Be very careful, Kelly. Wake up. Wake—

"—up." The word went off in her ear like an alarm.

It took her a couple of minutes to figure out why she was lying on a bed that wasn't her own. She pressed her hands against her temples, called up the events of the past day— her mother leaning against the doorframe with her coat on, her blood-stained silk pajamas underneath—Jasper's insistence that they leave the hospital and come home.

And then the crazy weather, and those same dudes on motorcycles that had been hassling her at the club the other night. And smashed the restaurant and the memorial because they were pissed at Jasper and acting like children. And something else? Something . . . ? She frowned and rubbed her temples. It felt as if that mist outside the windows had found its way inside her skull; there was something she felt she should remember, yet the mist had drifted over those memories, concealing them. She was probably just being paranoid. Why was Jasper slumped against the windowsill like that, his head in his arms? She thought he was sleeping, but she was wrong; he opened one eye and looked steadily at her. Images flitted in her skull, like moths going crazy around a porch light—something about a man with wings, but that couldn't be right.

"It was all just a dream, right?" she said to Jasper. She sat up on the bed and pushed her hands through her hair, raking it back from her face.

He gave her a small, crooked smile. "I guess that depends," he said, "on what you were dreaming. You were out cold for a while."

"What time is it?"

He checked his watch. "Going on nine in the morning."

"Feels earlier than that."

"It's the weather." Framed within the open window was a patch of overcast sky, a gray and empty street. "It's gotten warmer, though."

"Have you been there all night?"

He gave a slight nod.

"What have you been doing?"

Jasper rose and turned away from her as he mumbled something that sounded like ". . . making sure you're okay."

Kelly plucked at her lower lip, feeling like everything had been tilted just a little off balance. Wasn't there something she should be remembering? "There were people at the windows last night," she said suddenly. "They broke the windows, right?"

"Yeah." Half turning, so that his feet still pointed at the door, Jasper stared at her and frowned. He twisted the rest of himself in her direction. "What did you think of what happened last night?"

"What?"

"What exactly do you remember?"

For some reason she was annoyed, even though just moments ago she'd been asking the same thing of herself. "Just—" She waved a hand, gesturing at everything and nothing at the same time. "The windows," she said again.

"And Archie?"

"Who's Archie?"

He looked at her for a long moment, frown lines threading his forehead. "Well, hell. Maybe it's for the best." He spoke so low and so quickly she wasn't entirely sure she'd heard right.

"What's for the best?" There was a low, painful thumping in her skull. "Wow," she muttered, pushing her hands up through her hair again and staring down at the rumpled duvet. The sentence slipped out without her realizing. "Maybe my head's just messed up from bad E."

"What?"

Her brother's tone was sharp. Kelly's gaze jerked toward him, saw the dismay and disapproval written so clearly in his features, and tried to remember exactly what she had said. For some reason her thoughts, her speech, didn't entirely feel her own. She shook her head, trying to shake away the sensation, but it persisted.

"Kelly," Jasper was saying. "You took ecstasy? When?"

"Just—" She shrugged. Did they really need to talk about this? "Do we really need to talk about this?"

"Has this been, like, a regular thing or something?"

"Kind of."

"Kind of?"

"Oh, c'mon," she said crossly. "It's not like I'm some crack whore or anything. It's just, you know. It's just a bit of E now and then. With friends."

"Oh, Kel." He sighed and dropped onto the edge of the bed. "You should just leave that shit—all of it—you should just leave it alone."

"It's no big deal."

"It is a big deal. It's all lies. Okay? The stuff plays tricks with your mind and makes you think you're all happy and blissful when you're not. Makes you think that nothing's wrong, everything's fine, everybody loves you and everybody's your friend—"

"Isn't that the point?"

"—when they're not. When they might be out to take something from you, or hurt you, or just change their minds about you once they sober up." He stopped, as if realizing he'd gone someplace he hadn't intended. "The most important thing is to face the truth in your life," he said slowly. "You need to always know the truth. You can't accept lies and mind games. Or else you get tricked into the wrong kind of places."

"The abyss," Kelly said suddenly.

He looked startled by her choice of word.

"It's what you said last night in the car home," Kelly reminded him. "The abyss."

"Yeah," he muttered. "The abyss. The fucking void."

"So is that where you were all this time?"

He didn't answer. He looked so tired that her heart broke a little bit for him. He was looking at her as if he'd never truly seen her before. She recognized that expression on his face. She said, "You're looking at my scars."

"I'm just happy to see them so faded."

"Why do they bother you so much?"

"They don't."

"They do. They always have. I always noticed."

He looked out the window, shrugged. "'Cause it's my fault you got them."

"But—" She couldn't read his expression. His face had turned into a mask again. *A Jasper-mask,* she thought, *him but not really him.* "But you saved me. You pulled the dog off me. You even got that bite in your arm and they had to—"

"Kel," he said and sighed loudly. "I was the reason that dog got on you in the first place. Mom and Dad told me to watch you and I was reading a paperback. You wandered around the back of the gas station and—"

He stopped talking. He was staring down the street, looking for any signs of the people who vandalized their windows last night. He looked so worried. Why wasn't she feeling more worried? She had the nagging feeling she should be—more than worried, terrified—except she felt kind of lighthearted and chatty, even if he had annoyed her with that lecture about the E.

"I think they're really gone," Jasper said. "At least for now."

"Do you think they'll come back?"

He sighed and dragged a hand across his eyes, rubbed the corners. "I didn't think they'd come here at all. I think I made a horrible mistake." He looked at her again and then touched, very lightly, the scar at the corner of her mouth.

Their family had gone on a cross-country trip and stopped for car repair in the middle of nowhere—some hot midwestern state where the air felt scratchy in her throat and yellow fields rolled on forever. Kelly remembered that. She remembered Dad arguing with the mechanic and Mom going across the street to buy snacks. "I'm bored," she told her brother, but he was leaning against the car and reading a paperback, the cover folded back.

Jasper grunted, said, "Read that comic book I gave you."

But Kelly wasn't interested in comic books.

There had been a dog chained to a pole in the yard. He was skinny, sprawled in the dirt, his tongue hanging out, an empty metal bowl at his side. Kelly thought he looked lonely and decided to go over and say hello and give him a pat. She liked dogs.

She had no real memory of what happened next. She remembered the hospital, the emergency room, the look on her mother's face as the doctor sewed up the wound in Kelly's cheek, the other one near her mouth.

Now, Kelly said, "You pulled that dog off me. You got a nasty bite on your arm. You were, like, a hero."

He shrugged. "What the hell did you know? You were five."

"Six."

"You were five. See? You don't even remember that right. But the way Mom and Dad looked at me when they realized what I had—you were under my watch—"

Under my watch. It struck her as an odd phrase, not the kind he would normally say.

"—and I was in charge of you for a lousy half hour. And I forgot about where you were or what you were doing because I was too involved with my book. Everybody knew what happened to you was my fault—who would let a five-year-old wander right up to a chained-up junkyard dog? Everybody knew what could have happened to you, how bad it could have—"

"But it's okay," she said. "It turned out okay."

"So I knew I couldn't," he said. "I mean, in the hospital, when I overheard the doctor say *coma* and I knew that Mom and Dad would—that look in their eyes, the dog attack multiplied a hundred billion times, I knew I couldn't—"

She said, "What are you talking about? What coma?"

Jasper got off the bed. "Hungry," he said, and moved toward the door.

Kelly followed. "But I want to hear more about—"

"Forget it, Kel. I'm done talking."

He was halfway down the stairs and she was right behind him when something rushed at her from her dream in a stream of white mist, an animal with brown-gold eyes. Strangely intelligent eyes. Before she even knew what she was about to say, the words came out of her: "Did you help a coyote?"

The question to her own ears sounded absurd. She wasn't sure what had triggered it. Something about a dream, yes, and—now she remembered the coyote in the woods, the coyote sitting beneath the streetlamp the night Jasper had appeared. She watched Jasper for his expression, expecting him to laugh at her the way he had when they were little and she asked him her little-kid questions—"Why are dog's lips so wrinkly and floppy?"—although, after insulting her once or twice, he would try to answer them as seriously and thoroughly as he was able.

But now she was struck by the silence that followed her question, filled with the things he didn't say: *Help a what? Where the hell did that come from? Why would I help a— what was it you said? A coyote?*

That shadow passed through his eyes again, turning his face into a stranger's.

"You do ask the most unexpected questions," he said, just as someone rang the doorbell and pounded on the door.

CHAPTER ELEVEN

"Ruland! Hey, Ru-land! Open up!"

Jasper cocked his head. "Oh, I don't believe it," he said and a smile broke across his face.

He jumped the last three steps to the floor. He opened the door and a sandy-haired guy in jeans and a duffle coat, about eighteen or nineteen—Jasper's age—filled the door-frame. "Hey, Ruland, what up?" His craggy face looked familiar, but it was his voice that Kelly recognized—it was slow, drawling and cracked as if he'd already put in fifty years of drinking whiskey and smoking cigarettes.

"And there's the girl Ruland," Dan said, grinning up at her. She was still standing high on the staircase. Dan switched his attention back to her brother: "Put it here, man," he said, offering Jasper his hand and pulling him into a bear hug, thumping him on the back in a way that struck Kelly as painful. "Guess what? Came back from the West Coast yesterday afternoon . . . my brother's getting married, right, trapped some poor lass into marrying him . . ." That was another thing Kelly remembered about Dan: he liked using British and Irish phrases even though he'd never left the U.S. Dan was the kind of guy who gestured wildly as he talked and never seemed to know he was doing it. He was wearing black fingerless gloves. He took off the duffle coat but left the gloves on. ". . . and I hear this rumor, that ol' Jazzy has returned from wherever it was he went. Right? So I'm up early 'cause I'm jet-lagged all to hell and so I say to myself, Well, dude, let's go investigate this rumor. And look. Here you are." He beamed as if Jasper was a rabbit that Dan had pulled from a hat. "What the fuck happened to the windows?"

"Yeah, don't take off your shoes," Jasper said instead of answering. "There's broken glass everywhere."

"No shit. So what happened?"

"Someone broke them."

"Someone *disintegrated* them, is more like it. Dude—"

"I don't want to talk about it. I'm glad to see you." Kelly could sense Jasper's conflict. Part of her wanted Dan to hang out and make them feel like part of the normal world again. The other part wanted him to get the hell out, because what they were dealing with wasn't something to be shared.

A man with wings? Something about a man with—

With Jasper, at least, the first part won out. He said, "You want coffee?"

Dan looked around him, into the living room off one side and the dining room off the other. He looked at the windblown curtains and scattered. Kelly saw the questions on his face, then saw him consciously decide to put those questions to the side and just go with the flow. Whatever this thing was with the glass, it was not like it was *his* problem.

"Ah, that's what I remember about this family," Dan said as he followed Jasper down the hall into the kitchen. Broken glass crunched beneath his boots. "Always making coffee." They disappeared into the kitchen.

Kelly opened the front door and stepped onto the porch. She looked down the street in both directions, like she'd seen Jasper do upstairs. No one. Only mist, only weak watery sunlight filtering through dirty clouds. She felt uneasy. The window thing was really bothering her. She tried to remember more details about who had broken them and how they'd been broken and could not. What were they going to tell their parents? Why wasn't Jasper more concerned? He almost looked as if he just didn't care anymore, in the kitchen letting Dan talk his ear off as if everything was normal.

She went upstairs, tugged on a hoodie, and located her cell phone. The first person she called was her mother. Hannah said that she and the babies were good. She'd be in the hospital for observation for another couple of days; they wanted to make sure all her contractions had stopped. "They're so little I can't even feel them," she said. "But I'm hooked up to a machine that says I'm having them, so we have to make sure they don't develop into labor."

Kelly paused, on the verge of saying something about the house. Wanting to prepare her, feeling like she should. But she didn't want to inflict this on her mother. "Here," Hannah said suddenly, "your father wants to say hi."

Robert came on the line. "What's up, darlin'?"

She didn't know what to say to him, either. She didn't see how they could hide this or cover it up—they could clean up the mess, but the total absence of glass in the first-floor windows would not go unnoticed. It wasn't their fault, but why did she feel like telling anybody what had happened would only get Jasper in trouble? So maybe let Jasper take the lead in handling this? Give him time enough to figure something out?

She said good-bye to her father and hung up.

She called Nick. She tried to think of a reason, then confessed, "I just kind of wanted to hear your voice. I hope that doesn't sound too clingy or anything."

"No, it doesn't sound clingy." He was yawning into the phone.

"It's going to be a really bad day," she said, thinking about how her father would respond to the windows.

"How come?"

"Just—" She didn't have the energy to go into it. "Stuff."

"You want to come over here, hang for a bit?"

"I don't think I should leave my brother."

"He's a big boy."

"I just don't think I should leave him. I'll talk to you later, okay?"

"Kelly," he said, but she ended the call.

She was hungry. That, at least, she could fix. She could fix something for Jasper as well.

In the kitchen, Dan was asking her brother, who didn't seem to be fully listening: ". . . been in touch with the crew? You know they're dying to see you, right? They love you, man."

Jasper yawned. Dan was already pulling his cell phone from his back pocket and dancing his thumbs across the buttons. "Wait," Jasper said.

"The house is destroyed anyway, what with the windows and everything, so why don't we have some people over? Celebrate your return. Can't believe you haven't done that yet."

"This isn't a good time."

"It's always a good time."

"Dan." Jasper reached out and wrapped his hand around the cell phone. "No. I have to take Kelly somewhere else anyway. We won't be staying at the house today."

"I'm making breakfast burritos," Kelly said to shift Dan's attention. "Dan, you want one? Or," she said, as Jasper made a slashing motion at his throat, "maybe you need to get going."

"I'd love a burrito," Dan said.

"Sure, but it'll have to be quick," Jasper said. "Kelly and I need to get going."

Kelly assumed he meant the hospital, but suddenly wondered if he meant something else. *If you stay close to me they can't touch you.* The phrase came back to her from the other night. He had said that to her, right? About the people who broke the windows?

"Where are you headed?" Dan asked and was distracted by Mojo, who had always had a good relationship with him.

She appeared from wherever she'd been hiding, standing on her hind legs and putting her paws on his chair in greeting. "Sweet puppy," Dan said and picked her up and gave her a cuddle.

Jasper poured himself a coffee and looked out the window. Checking.

The doorbell rang just as Kelly was wrapping up the final burrito. Mojo was barking madly at the front door, although it didn't seem to occur to her that she could trot right through the living room windows if she wanted. Wondering who it could be and how she could get rid of them, Kelly opened the door and came face-to-face with Nick.

"Hi," he said. "The windows."

"Don't ask. Please don't ask," she said. She lifted her eyebrows. "I wasn't expecting you."

"I know. I just thought I'd drop by. You sounded strange on the phone and Sam and I decided to go out for pancakes anyway. Mom went into the city so I'm on big brother duty."

Mojo dashed out onto the front lawn. Sam, Nick's little brother, came running out from behind Truck. "Hi, Kelly!" he yelled. "Hi, Mojo!" Mojo leaped and danced with joy and Sam fell to his knees and scratched Mojo's neck and ears. "Want to play?" Sam said. "Wouldja like that?"

"Sam," Kelly called. "Just keep Mojo in the side yard and keep the gate shut, okay?"

Mojo was running after Sam with her favorite squeaky mouse toy, appealing to him to throw it for her. "Okay," Sam called and took Mojo through the gate into the side yard. Sam was ten, with brown curly hair and a small wiry body. He loved soccer and had a collection of T-shirts with sayings on them. He threw the toy and Mojo barked with glee and ran after it. Kelly took Nick to the edge of the porch and they sat on the swing to keep an eye on the dog and the boy.

"So I wanted to stop by," Nick said, "because I get the feeling that things are really weird."

Kelly sighed and leaned forward and put her head in her hands.

"They are, aren't they?" Nick said.

"Interesting that you didn't say *wrong*. You said *weird*."

"But they're wrong, too. Right? They've felt wrong for months."

Kelly rested her chin on her knee. "Yes," she said. "So you've felt it all this time, too, and never said anything?"

"I couldn't make sense of the feeling. It wasn't logical so I decided I was just being stupid. Or that it was your own anxiety kind of leaking onto me. Because you were constantly talking about that night, you know, about how it feels wrong in your head."

"Because I can't remember it."

"Yeah."

"You always gave the sensible explanation," she said. "But now you've changed your mind."

"Since Jasper came back, yeah. After the weird thing with the guy at the memorial. It got me thinking. Because things have been weird since the night of the rave," Nick said. "I can't shake this feeling that life after the rave went in one direction when it actually should have gone in another. Like somehow that night things got jumbled around, you know, like pieces from different puzzles getting into the wrong boxes. I told you it doesn't make sense. But it's been *bugging* me."

"The rave," Kelly said again. "The rave that neither of us went to."

"True," Nick said. He paused. Then he said, "Because I can't shake this feeling that you and I. That. Well. That we hooked up that night."

"Nick." She looked at him, laughed. "We did no such thing."

"I know that," he said. "I know that. In my head."

"But your heart says something else?" She was sarcastic.

"Not my heart," he said. "My gut. Look, I know I was home that night. I know you really wanted to go to that thing but got grounded after you and Morgan lied your way out of a field trip and went to a mall instead."

"It was a stupid field trip," she muttered. "Pointless."

"But we had just moved and Mom was still a mess from the custody battle and I promised her I wouldn't go because she just didn't have a good feeling about it. That's what she said. 'Not a good feeling.' But I didn't care either way—I never got the point of that music anyway and I can't stand crowds when I don't know anybody, so—"

"And yet we hooked up there," Kelly said. "Even though we didn't go there. Is that what you're saying?"

"I don't know what I'm saying. But I feel like we really did hook up. And it's been bothering me for a long time. And I'm only telling you this now because you seem to be going through such weird shit, with your brother coming back and all that, that this seems pretty mundane in comparison. What happened to the windows?"

They were distracted by a small barking shape hurtling across the front lawn and running down the street, into the mist.

"Mojo!" Kelly jumped to her feet.

"Sam," Nick said, turning on the small boy, who stood bewildered by the gate, "Kelly told you to—"

"I did! It was shut! I swear, I shut and locked the gate! I don't know how she got out!" The boy looked genuinely upset. "I'll go find her," he decided, and started trotting across the front lawn. "I'll fix it, don't worry."

"Sam," Kelly called, "don't. She's just running after a squirrel or going over to bark at our neighbor's Lab or something."

But the boy only broke into a run and before she could jump off the porch after him, or even call out for him to stop, he had taken off down the street, the mist swirling around him. "I'll get her!" he yelled, his voice frantic. "I'll get her before she gets hit by a car!"

Nick sighed. "Sam's beagle got hit by a Volvo six months ago, remember?"

"We should go after him," Kelly said. "Before he goes too far."

"Kelly, it's not like he's in mortal danger or anything. He's just really worried."

"Let's go for a walk," Kelly said. The sentence just slipped out from her. She had the feeling of something slithering through her brain, something that didn't quite belong there. *A man with wings,* she thought again, looking down the street. A man with wings? Something weird about his eyes, going right into her brain?

He's in your head, Kelly. Be careful.

Who had said that to her?

Jasper had said, "Whatever happens, stay close to me. They can't touch you if you stay close to me."

Go inside and get him and look for Sam together, Kelly thought and was about to do just that when she heard herself say, "Let's go for a walk." And then she was crossing the yard to the street as any other option vanished from her head.

It felt good to be moving, good to be outside. The air was sharp and fresh from last night's rain. The mist drifted in the street and she caught motion inside it.

"Sam!" Nick yelled.

Footsteps somewhere ahead of them, a small boy's voice calling out, "Where's Mojo? I don't see Mojo!"

"She's around," Kelly assured him, but an odd feeling was sliding around inside her again. They shouldn't have left the house. She shouldn't have strayed so far from Jasper, although she couldn't figure out why she would feel that way. She was a big girl, for crying out loud. Besides, they needed to find Mojo. Just because the dachshund was sensible and knew the neighborhood and shied away from anything that got close enough to seem a threat—a car, another dog, a person, even a squirrel, if it was big and aggressive enough—didn't mean that something couldn't happen to her.

To distract herself, she started talking about the first thing that came into her head. Which turned out to be her mother, how she had ended up in the hospital and how long it had taken to find the second baby's heartbeat. She was babbling a bit and could hear the nervousness in her voice as the mist slipped and shifted around them, but Nick listened all the same. "It was scary," she said. "The look on my mom's face . . . they're not even born yet and already she's so protective of them."

"That's not so surprising," Nick said.

"I just never really thought about it before."

"About what? Babies?"

Kelly flapped a hand. A useless gesture, she realized, but in moments like this things seemed blocked up inside her and it was tough to put them into words. "Kind of everything, maybe," she said. Then: "The babies, yeah. They weren't real to me before. It's not like I could imagine myself as a person with younger siblings. I mean, I'm the younger sibling. I've always been the protected one. Not the one who does the protecting."

She stopped walking as she said this. She felt like she'd just realized something about herself.

Nick said, "Sam can be a real pain in the ass, like now, for example, but he also worships the ground I walk on. Which is cool, you know. It's not like anybody else is gonna do that."

"I think I could handle being worshiped."

"I think you'll deal with it well."

They resumed walking. Sam was in sight now, crisscrossing the street up in front of them, yelling Mojo's name. Other than that, it was quiet. The air felt damp and cool. Kelly felt the need to start talking again. "He's not the same, you know. He's changed."

Nick was silent.

"Jasper," Kelly clarified. "Some of the things he says now . . ."

"Like what?"

"He talks about *the abyss*." She remembered another phrase Jasper had used. "*The void*. You ever hear anybody say things like that? I mean, like, in the course of daily conversation? I mean, someone who wasn't—"

"Crazy?"

"Yeah," she said. "But Jasper's not crazy."

"I didn't say he was."

"But I don't know what's scarier. Either we're crazy and the world around us is normal, or we're normal and the world around us is crazy."

"Or maybe there's no normal," Nick said. "Maybe it's all just different kinds of crazy."

She hitched in a breath, considered this. "No," she decided. "That's not a reassuring option."

Nick glanced at her.

"I think you're right," Kelly said slowly. "About the hooking up thing. Because I always thought it was strange that we didn't. I wanted to. I thought you wanted to. But it's like we just woke up one morning and that desire was gone."

"That desire was not gone," Nick said. "Not for me, anyway. I just couldn't—I didn't—like I said, I couldn't make sense of it. It gave me a really uneasy feeling. So I just kind of shut it down for a while."

She thought back to when Nick had first showed up in the halls of their high school: a sandy-haired, hazel-eyed boy with a shy smile and a wary gaze. He'd come from the city, people said, his mother had divorced his big-shot lawyer father and taken Nick and his younger brother out of private school and moved them here, where it was supposed to be healthier. That was the word she had used, at least according to one girl who had heard it from her mother who had heard it from the woman herself: *healthier,* and Kelly imagined an ominous tone to the word, as if the town was some kind of vegetable stir-fry Nick was supposed to choke down or else.

Kelly thought he was cute from the start, but it wasn't just that. Nick was independent. You could see it in the way he moved through all the kids, the different cliques, affable and confident but also aloof in a way that reminded Kelly of her brother. He wasn't looking to attach himself to any one group or the kind of identity that a group would give him. He didn't even seem to be looking for friends, not particularly; it was as if the school was a new car he was taking for a test drive, not ready yet to commit. Then he became a photographer for the school paper, started eating lunch regularly with some of the smart artsy kids. A couple of those kids were

Kelly's friends, as well, which gave her the perfect point of connection to him, since he wasn't in any of her classes.

He had had an open, soft-eyed way of looking at her that she could feel all the way down to her toes. Soon he was all she could think about. They sought each other out in the hallways, the cafeteria, the school lawn, the parking lot; the kids who were still her friends then cracked wise, knowing comments, but Kelly always denied, denied, denied. She didn't want to talk about her growing attraction to Nick. It was the first secret she had ever felt compelled to keep from her friends, as if talking about it would somehow render it . . . ordinary . . . just another thing that people could roll their eyes at and mock. When she was with Nick, she imagined them carving out their own little pocket of space and time, where she could start fresh and be somebody new. Or maybe not new, just . . .

Better.

Stronger, smarter, more confident, someone who wasn't so needy of her friends' approval or her older brother's attention.

"And then it all disappeared," Kelly murmured.

She didn't realize she'd actually spoken aloud until she noticed Nick staring at her. She'd been so intensely wrapped up in her own thoughts that seeing his flesh-and-blood presence right there, right in front of her, startled her a little. It was as if she'd been disappearing into her own mind, her memory. *God, what is happening to me?*

"You're right," she said to Nick. "We were going to hook up. We were . . ." She could feel her face turning red, and she looked away, hoping he hadn't noticed. "When I first met you I liked you. I thought you were cute. But something happened to that."

"After the rave? I would see you in the hall," Nick continued, "and I would feel kind of . . . strange. Dizzy. I always hid it, you know, dismissed it, but it was always there. Like this weird dark thing was closing over me."

"This wrongness," Kelly said suddenly. "This void. Like Jasper said. That's what it is, isn't it? What he's talking about. What you're talking about right now. And even my—my anxiety attacks—what if it's all connected, Nick? What if it's all part of the same thing? What if it—"

She stopped, unsure of what she'd been about to say.

Except that wasn't true. She knew what she was going to say—

What if it goes back, all of it, to that rave in the valley? The night of the accident? To something Jasper did, or didn't do—

She just couldn't bring herself to say it.

"Kel," he said. "You lost me. What are you talking about?"

"The void," she said again, starting to feel a bit frantic. "The abyss—"

"Forget the damn abyss," Nick muttered—

—and she shut up, because then he was kissing her.

His lips touched hers, softly, and she stood on her tiptoes and fitted herself against him, and they stood like that for what seemed a very long while. It started out as a gentle, easy kiss, and she was amazed at how comfortable it was, as if they instinctively knew how to move into each other; there was no scraping of teeth or awkward bumping or the wrong kind of tongue movement that secretly repelled her. Nick kissed the same way he spoke: slow, drawling, as if he had all the time in the world and didn't need to be anywhere other than where he was standing right then. When the kiss got more serious, when she felt a kind of liquid heat spreading through her body and she could feel herself craving more of him in a way that made her anxious and nervous, she pulled back and stepped away, then grinned at him in an effort to disguise just how rattled she was. His own eyes were bright and he looked rumpled and sheepish . . . but pleased.

"Nice move," she said.

"Thanks," he said. "I got it from a movie."

"Wait. Did you hear that?"

After a moment, the sound came again: a low-pitched whimper unlike any sound that Kelly had ever heard Mojo make. But when she stepped onto the lawn and pushed aside some bushes she saw the dachshund, curled up in the hedge as if she were hoping it might swallow her, a dash of red against the green. She was trembling. "Mojo," Kelly said. The dog studied her with large brown eyes, as if to assure herself it was actually Kelly; then she slithered out from the hedge, her belly flattened against the earth, her tail tucked between her legs. "Oh, Mojo!" Kelly said and scooped her up and cradled the dog against her chest. Mojo chuffed and licked her hand. After a moment, the dog's trembling stopped.

"Something scared the hell out of her," Nick said. And then, "Sam?"

Kelly tightened her hold on the dog.

"Sam!" Nick strode into the street. "Sam!"

Only silence. Mist swirled through the trees, roamed the sidewalks, enveloped Nick's long lean form so that, for a moment, he disappeared from Kelly's view. She stepped forward, squeezing the dog so tightly that Mojo yelped, and Nick reemerged again, but this swath of mist kept thickening. As she made a slow turn and gazed in all directions, she saw no sign of the shaggy-haired ten-year-old. Only the empty broken pavement and the trees lining both sides, branches making naked twisted shapes in the air. The mist eddied and flowed.

"I don't understand where he could have gone," Nick said. His voice was tight. "He was just here."

"I think . . ." Kelly said, when the sound of footsteps caught their attention.

The hazy outline of a man appeared through the mist, then seemed to neatly detach from it. Or rather, Kelly thought wildly, it was as if the mist folded itself *away* from him, as if out of a kind of reverence.

The man, tall and slender and pale, held someone in his arms. The figure of a boy, his legs and arms gone limp, his head thrown back and dangling.

"I know you," Kelly heard herself say and then it was as if something in her brain dislodged itself, and memory could flow again. The man in the woods, the man in the classroom, the man in the street last night. *With the wings.* But that couldn't have been possible, must have been some kind of weird hallucination on her part—a trick of the light, or the mind—

In any case, there was no sign of them now.

"Archie," Kelly said.

"Sweet thing," Archie greeted her. "Nick. Nicky. How're you?"

Nick said, "Who the hell are—" But then his voice fell silent and Kelly saw recognition move through his features. The man from the woods.

Archie inclined his head toward Kelly, as if deflecting the question to her.

"Look who I found." Archie's voice was like velvet. "They're such angels when they're sleeping. So are you looking out for Sam, Nick, the way Jasper's been looking out for little sis? Isn't that what you people need to do, in a world big and bad as this one?" His voice turned sly, mocking. "Don't you need to look out for each other?"

"Give him back to me," Nick said.

Archie's eyes were burning. But his voice was diamond cold. "Say please."

Kelly touched Nick's sleeve. Nick was motionless, his gaze locked on Archie, trying, Kelly knew, to figure out what kind of person he was dealing with here.

"Please," Nick said.

"Sure." Sudden warmth in Archie's voice, as if they were old friends, joshing around. With what seemed exaggerated care, he set the boy on his feet and kissed him on the forehead. Kelly couldn't help flinching at the contact, but Sam only opened his eyes and gave his head a slight shake. He took a long moment to look around him. Then he hitched in a breath and ran to his brother, crashing into Nick's legs.

"Sam," Kelly said quickly, kneeling in front of him. "I have a job for you. I need you to take Mojo and get her back to the house. As fast as possible. I really need you to do this. Okay?"

"Who are these people?"

"I need you to do what I said. Okay?"

"You guys come, too," Sam said. "You and Nick come, too."

"We need to have ourselves a conversation first," Archie said. "Go now. Before I change my mind. Cute thing like you might get all eaten up."

"Go," Nick whispered and Sam backpedaled away from all of them, cradling Mojo tightly against his chest. Then he turned and walked, very quickly and stumbling, toward the house.

The mist swallowed him whole.

It was then that Kelly clicked into something Sam had said:

Who are these people?

Not just Archie.

And now, turning slowly, she saw.

There were other figures moving inside the mist. "C'mon, Nick," she muttered, "let's just get out of here," when a Rider stepped out in front of them, tall and lean in tattered dark blue leather, dark hair framing a face that looked . . . wrong, somehow. Too gaunt, and too . . . *smooth,* Kelly realized, like the skin had been buffed to a high, unnatural polish. His eyes glittered.

She turned to her right but another Rider had appeared

there, blocking her. This one was shorter than the other, with wider shoulders and a smaller face with features that seemed squished together, but the uncanny light in the eyes and sheen to the skin were the same. He grinned.

"I think we should talk," Archie said quietly.

She forced herself to look at him.

"Why don't you come with us," Archie said, "just for a while, and together I think we can talk—or maybe knock—some sense into that brother of yours."

"I—" Kelly said and suddenly Riders were everywhere, surging out of the mist, the air ringing with footsteps; it was almost like a special effect in a movie, where one person had magically multiplied into dozens. Two Riders stepped out from behind Archie and came toward her. The taller one wore a leather duster coat, had spurs on his boots that jangled as he walked. The other one had a long black network of braids and a wide carnivorous smile.

"You see," Archie was saying, as Kelly felt a presence moving up behind her, felt long cold fingers grip her shoulder, "I'm getting so tired—"

"Don't touch her!"

The explosion of his voice was so unfamiliar it took her a second to realize it was Nick, *her* Nick, attacking the Rider who had grabbed her. She felt pressure on her shoulders as she was dragged back several steps and then suddenly she was free. She whirled around to see that Nick had both arms wrapped round the Rider's neck in a chokehold, the Rider in the tattered blue leather.

"Nick," Kelly yelled—

—because suddenly Archie was standing right beside Nick, even though just a moment ago he had been at least twenty feet away. "We can't have this," Archie said. Nick glanced over in surprise and Archie's hand flashed at his face. Nick's head jerked back in impact and he crumpled, the Rider stepping clear of him and flashing a look at Kelly. The Rider's eyes were laced with red, a shocking contrast to the smooth, snow-white skin.

Archie was crouching beside Nick, who lay sprawled on the pavement. He grabbed a handful of Nick's hair and pulled back his head. For a moment Kelly panicked that he was about to cut Nick's throat, except he had no knife in hand. Nick's eyes were closed. Archie saw her watching, said, "Don't move, sweetie, or this could get ugly." She wasn't sure she *could* move. Archie locked eyes with her a moment longer, then lowered his head and whispered into the ear of the unconscious boy. The whispering seemed to go on forever. Nothing moved. Nothing breathed.

Then Archie let go of Nick's head and stood up.

"As I was saying," he said. "I'm tired of this. We're all tired. I want to move on." He spread his hands. "My boys want to move on. That's how it works. To stop is to die. And your family needs to move on, as well. Mind if I smoke?" A cigarette had appeared between Archie's fingers. He admired it for a moment. "I will give you people credit where credit is due," he muttered. "This is a very nice vice." Archie took a drag on the cigarette, even though Kelly didn't understand how he could have lit it. He blew smoke through his nostrils and looked directly at her. "This is all your brother's fault," he said. "Well, to get technical about it, I suppose it's all yours."

"My fault?"

"But it would have happened anyway. After all, I watch and I wait. That's what I do. And I have all the time in the world. More, even."

"What are you talking about? Could you tell me what's going on? And how—"

Archie lifted one blond eyebrow. "How?"

She licked her lips. They were dry and cracked. "How we can make you go away?"

"But that's the thing. It's so *easy*. All you have to do is give me what I want, give me what I'm owed, and I'm gone. Just like that." Archie snapped his fingers. "I'm like a bill collector. Not your favorite person, maybe, but easy enough to make go away. All you need to do is pay up." Then he smiled a little and said, "Right, Jasper?"

Silence.

But Archie turned and then Kelly heard new footsteps in the mist. Jasper wore jeans and his favorite zippered sweatshirt, and as he lifted his hands and drew back the hood Kelly flashed on the thought: *He's started to look like them. The Riders.*

He's turning into one of them.

The uncanny, moon-pearl sheen to his skin. The gleam of his eyes. And his ever-thinning body: as if Archie had taken an invisible blade to him, to all of them, carving away vital flesh until they were these stripped-down ghosts of themselves. *Like wraiths,* Kelly thought. *Wraiths on motorcycles.*

Jasper said in a low voice, "It won't happen here, Archie."

"It doesn't have to. Just so long as it happens."

"What?" Kelly cried. "What happens?"

"Your brother and I made a deal," Archie said. "I fulfilled my end. But your brother deserted us—" Archie touched a hand to his chest, as if the thought was genuinely painful. "—before he could give me all that I am owed. Jasper, Jasper." Archie shook his head. "What did you think was going to happen? What did Cairo tell you? That if you just waited me out, I would go my merry way and take my little band with me?"

"Something like that." Jasper cleared his throat. "He said it had happened before."

"But that was only when I didn't *care*. Sometimes I'm wrong, Jasper. Sometimes I choose a soul and it . . . turns out to be a little *off*. I'm not perfect. I do make mistakes. But *your* soul, Jasper. Your soul is . . . a beautiful, tasty thing. And I mean to collect the rest of it. Are we clear?"

"Crystal," Jasper said. His face was smooth and impossible to read. "But you need to leave my sister out of it."

"But she's so tied up *in* it," Archie said. "She goes all *through* it. It starts and *ends* with her. So how am I supposed to do that?" He threw out his hands, as if in exasperation. "Seriously, I'd love to know."

Jasper unzipped his sweatshirt and slipped it off his body.

Kelly gasped.

Jasper stood in the middle of the street, naked to the waist.

The night of his homecoming, Kelly had glimpsed the tattoos—or whatever they were, because she had never seen tattoos like this—along his upper arm, the dense and intricate arabesques.

Now she saw that they covered his torso completely. It was as if they had erased his own skin and formed one of their own: a strange, alien skin made up of different shades of ink: dark and gray and silvery pale, casting off their own strange glow into the foggy street.

And as Kelly watched, some of the marks began to . . .

. . . to writhe . . . to move . . . crawling across his shoulders, moving up and down his arms . . .

A collective hissing, sighing sound rippled through the circle of Riders and some of them started falling back into the fog, disappearing. Kelly heard motorcycles kicking into life, disappearing down the street. Jasper continued to stand there, his head tilted to the side, as if he was staring into space and dreaming; he was letting his new, strange skin do the speaking for him. And whatever it was saying—whatever language it was using—or spell it was casting—was having an effect. The Riders were falling away, vanishing, leaving them alone.

Except for Archie.

Even as she watched, he seemed to be expanding, his arms and legs lengthening as if to command the entire street. Behind him, shadows slipped like sharks through the fog and the air thrummed with the sound of engines, reeked of gasoline.

"You can't touch him," Kelly yelled.

And it wasn't just a stupid stubborn cry on her part; it was *true*. She saw that. The marks on Jasper's body were like a shield that protected him, held him apart.

"Cairo and his damned spell of protection," Archie said. The wind blew back his white-blond hair. His eyes blazed. "We had a deal, son. I gave you yours." The voice changed, like liquid hardening into rock. "Now give me mine."

Kelly heard Jasper take a breath.

"Time to come home," Archie said.

Jasper replied, "I am home."

"Home," Archie said, "always changes. Sooner or later. I am your home now."

He held out his hand and perspective skewed; the air around him hazed, a fog within a fog, a ghostly aura; his arm kept unfolding and unfolding, like a never-ending jackknife, and his hand unfurled and his fingers cut through the air, the nails sharp and glinting like daggers. "Either you give me what is mine or I'll take little sis and stash her in some hellhole where she can scream for a million years and no one cares."

Then suddenly he was just a man again, standing in the middle of the road.

He and Jasper faced each other.

Showdown in the suburbs, Kelly thought, and bit down on a laugh that felt very much like hysteria.

"Jasper." Archie's voice had turned mild. "I know it's hard. You're caught in between things. You're no longer one of them, and you're not yet one of us. Walking around with half a soul is so much more painful than no soul at all. When you come back into the fold, my child, you'll see how quickly all that pain goes away. Just goes away."

"Not today, Archie."

"But soon." Archie was walking backward, away from them, smiling. "If you want me to wait, I'll wait. But we're bored. We'll have to find things to do." He shrugged. "I guess we can burn things. Then start to kill things. Let me know when you've seen the light."

He looked at Kelly, gave her a wink, and was gone.

CHAPTER TWELVE

They were all gone, retreating into mist, like waves slipping back into ocean.

"Jasper," Kelly said.

It took a moment for him to react to her voice. When he turned his head toward her, she saw the look in his eyes and she recoiled. A look of hunger. Longing.

He wants to go with them, she thought.

He wants to be riding again.

But then that look also faded and Jasper seemed more or less like himself again.

"We should go back," he said.

"Nick," she breathed.

How could she have forgotten about her friend, even for a moment? She spun toward the place he had fallen, where Archie had pulled up his head by the hair and whispered God knew what in his ear—

But he wasn't there.

"Nick?"

He didn't seem to be anywhere.

"Nick!"

Only empty street: the cracked and broken pavement, the gnarled maples and oaks, the sprawling yards of dead grass and hardpacked earth, the Victorian houses set way back from the sidewalk, behind the hedges and trees. Everything was quiet and shut down, even though it was a Saturday. As if people were keeping inside, hiding from the weather. Or maybe just hiding.

"He's probably back at the house," Jasper said. "His car is there, right?"

"Why wouldn't he wait for us?"

Jasper shrugged. "He took a blow to the head—"

"Exactly. What if he's just wandering around and needs help?"

"If he's not back at the house, and his car is still there, we'll send out a search party," Jasper said.

"They wouldn't have taken him, would they? Archie?"

"Archie's no real threat to Nick. He's not interested in Nick."

As he spoke a car hurtled around the corner and sped past them, too fast, so that Kelly leaped sideways onto the sidewalk. She was about to call out an insult when she recognized the back of Nick's battered truck, the back of his sandy-haired head at the wheel. Sam was in the cab beside him. Kelly felt a surge of relief . . . and then puzzlement.

"See?" Jasper said. "There he goes."

"But . . ."

Kelly stood there, staring after the car.

"Kelly. Come on."

The mist seemed to be thinning a little, but it still un-settled her; she thought she saw shapes flitting at the edges of her vision, but when she turned her head all she saw was a tree or telephone pole or gate blocking off somebody's driveway.

And she remembered what had been written at the scene of the trashed memorial: "My soul to take."

She turned to her brother, who saw the expression on her face and cut her off before she could speak.

"I know," Jasper said.

"He was—I mean, it's a kind of—it's a *metaphor,* right? Like in English lit. It's, like, code for something else. He's just saying that he owns you, or something, or—" She was bab-bling, she realized, but she couldn't seem to help it, couldn't stop talking. "He's— What is he? What is Archie?"

"Mig—one of the Riders, the one who got in that scuffle with Nick—once described him as a kind of fallen angel," Jasper said slowly. "Mig said he's from a whole other place and time."

"Another place and time," Kelly echoed blankly.

"Yeah, like there are all these different realities and the one we know is just a small part of—" Jasper sighed. "It's complicated. I still don't understand it. But the reality Archie was in? It didn't want him anymore. It kicked him out. So now he's here. Where he gathers his Riders around him."

"The Riders," Kelly said. "What are they? They don't seem—they don't seem fully—" She caught the tremble in her own voice because she noticed again her brother's gaunt face, the lean fluid grace of his body, the way he seemed to be turning . . . into something else.

Kelly made the connection—*About time,* a little voice chattered at the back of her head. *You're kinda slow at this, aren't you?* And she said, "Their souls. Archie took them. Took them all. Just like he's trying to take yours." She could feel herself starting to babble again.

"Archie didn't just take them," Jasper said. "He bought them."

"Bought them. Bought them? How can you—how is that—"

"He bargained for them."

"You mean people just—trade him their souls for something else? Like he's the devil or something?"

Jasper shrugged.

"But who would do that? Give up your soul like that?"

Jasper's voice turned dry as old bone. "Archie makes it hard to refuse."

She looked back at Jasper. It felt as if something had shifted inside her—something small, subtle, and yet she could feel the difference, as if her gaze had taken on an edge of clarity.

"What did you sell your soul for?" Kelly said.

Jasper acted as if he didn't hear, striding down the sidewalk. Kelly hurried after him. "You made a deal with him," she said again, her voice rising, "you traded your soul to that—that thing, that Archie thing—didn't you?"

"This isn't the time to discuss it."

"It's never the time to discuss this stuff with you! You won't *tell* me!"

Jasper whirled on her. She could see the muscles twitching in his face; his eyes were blazing. But then his face turned smooth and empty again—*the Jasper-mask,* she thought—and he turned away from her and resumed walking. The house was just up ahead. But Kelly wasn't ready to give up. She said, "What kind of deal did he make with *you*?"

"Not your business, Kelly."

"Archie seems to think it is."

"You trust Archie over me? Fine. Go ask him."

She stopped in her tracks.

He paused, his shoulders slumping a little in the hooded sweatshirt, and then he said without looking around at her, "I didn't mean it like that. You know that."

She was going to say something like, "That's okay," but she heard instead a completely different explosion of words: "You really think I could trust some loser like you? You had everything and you blew it. For what? To go party?"

She hadn't meant to say that. She had not. And then she was too shocked by those words to say anything. Jasper stopped and faced her. He didn't look hurt or angry or even annoyed; he was studying her carefully. And then more words were slipping out of her: "All you've done," she said, "is feed me one lie after another."

"I didn't lie to you."

"No. You omitted things. But that's just another form of lying."

Jasper said, "Is that really you talking, Kelly?" He took a step closer. "Archie can really get into your head, you know. So—"

But her gaze had gone beyond him to the driveway.

"Dad's home," she said.

But it wasn't the sight of her father's car that took out her knees so that her legs almost buckled. The driveway was filled with words, letters thin and jagged like chicken scratches, taking up every inch of pavement:

COME BACK TO US COME BACK TO US
COME BACK TO US COME BACK TO US
COME BACK . . .

CHAPTER THIRTEEN

Through the shattered windows, the blowing curtains, Kelly could see the shape of her father. He was looking out at them through the dining room window—or rather, through the space where the window had been—with his arms folded, his sleeves rolled up so you could see his tattoos. Kelly hugged herself. Every now and then Kelly could see him as other people must seem him and realize how physically intimidating he was.

Jasper sighed. His face was grim. Kelly was following him into the house when she paused at the front door. Written across it were the words:

I all alone beweep my outcast state

She yanked her jacket sleeve over her hand and swiped it across the sentence, changing it into a long smear of neon pink chalk. With dread, she went into the house. Robert and

Jasper had moved back into the living room and Robert was saying ". . . begin to explain just what happened here?"

"It wasn't Jasper's fault," Kelly blurted.

"The windows," Robert said. "The *windows*."

Jasper said, "I know. It's a mess."

"The windows, Jasper. The writing on the driveway. Just like at the bar. Done by the same people?"

"Yeah."

"So before obviously *wasn't* an isolated incident? Like you told me it would be?"

"No," Jasper said. "But I didn't know. I honestly didn't know. I thought things—would turn out differently."

For a moment Kelly thought her brother was going to hang his head, like when he was younger. But Jasper kept his gaze level with his father's, which seemed to irk Robert all the more.

"That was my mistake," Jasper said. "And I apologize."

"A mess," Robert said softly. "This is a real big mess, son. I don't know what trouble you got in or what the hell you brought back to this town with you, but there are other people involved in this now besides you. I have other people in this family to protect. You understand? So you need to be straight with me."

"Dad," Jasper said, "you couldn't believe me if I told you. You wouldn't even begin to know how."

"The police are on their way. You're going to talk to them. You're going to tell them everything you didn't tell them the last time."

"It won't help. Trust me on that."

"*Trust* you? I don't even *know* you anymore."

"Dad." Jasper's voice was flat and tired. "You never did."

Robert jerked his head back.

"Jasper," Kelly said, although she had no idea what she was going to say next.

He ignored her, turned his back on them both, and walked up the stairs.

That left Kelly staring at her father in the strange misty silence, the cold air moving through the house, shattered window glass gleaming on the floor.

Robert said, in a soft tone of voice that unnerved her more than anyone else's yelling ever did, "So what have you guys been up to, Kelly?" He lifted his hands a little. "I'm just trying to get some sort of understanding—"

"He's a bad influence, I guess."

The words just came out of her. *No,* Kelly thought. *No. I didn't mean to say that. That's not what I meant at all.* But it was like something had stirred inside her brain, some strange alien snake moving through her thoughts, shoving them aside to impose words of its own: "He's a bad influence," she heard herself say again.

Robert's eyes turned very grave, as if he'd been afraid of this all along.

"How so?" he said. "Kelly, does this have anything to do with drugs?"

It always comes back to drugs, she was thinking, even as she heard herself say in a voice that both was and was not her own: "Yeah. I've done ecstasy." Her voice felt wooden, jerky; it was like she'd been turned into a flesh-and-blood puppet; surely her father could see that? That this really wasn't her talking?

Archie can really get into your head.

"You know," Kelly went on, unable to make herself stop, "MDMA?"

"I know what ecstasy is. You're saying you got it from your brother?"

"Wait—no." Kelly shook her head. She had to fight to assemble her thoughts into some kind of order, into something that felt like hers again. There was a fog in her head. "No, Dad, that's not what I meant at all." A relief to finally get the words out, her own words, but the expression on Robert's face didn't change.

He said, "So you were lying about your drug use?"

"No! I mean—Jasper had nothing to do with it. Jasper—"

"I'm no idiot, Kelly. I'm not blind. When Jasper started getting into—into the whole rave thing—"

"He never—"

"The music," Robert went on. "That whole subculture. I know what it involves. It's my fault—and maybe your mother's—for turning a blind eye to it, once he started dropping out of all his athletics and—"

"He dropped out of sports because he didn't like competing," Kelly said.

But she could tell from the look on her father's face that such a concept was beyond him.

"It had nothing to do with drugs," Kelly said. "And he's into the rave thing because he really likes the music. Look,

I know—" She took a breath. She was about to say things she had never said before, had never allowed herself to truly *think* before, and she let the words pour out of her before they could be hijacked by that strange snake-in-her-brain feeling again. "I know you had this wild messed-up youth," Kelly said, "and I know you don't like to talk about it, and I know you got in trouble with drinking and drugs and stuff before you, like, turned your life totally around, and I really respect that, and I know you look at Jasper and you worry—you worry about him because he seems like you in so many ways, but he isn't. You have to understand that. He isn't. This trouble he's in now—I don't understand it, but it's not—it's not about drugs—it's about something else completely—"

"Not just me," Robert said quietly. "You don't know my side of the family very well, Kelly, because your mother and I decided to keep you kids protected from all that—but there's a lot of—" His mouth worked silently for a moment and then he continued, "—addiction, alcoholism, that's caused a lot of damage. A lot of craziness. All through my family. It's like a gene that gets inherited—"

"Jasper's not the one you have to worry about." Did she really believe all this? She wasn't sure. But it was important that her father believe this. Jasper's life these days was difficult enough.

Robert said, "So maybe *you're* the one I should be worrying about? Is that what you're saying?"

"I—" She suddenly couldn't take the weight of her father's gaze. "I don't know what I'm saying," she mumbled, and before she could risk saying anything else she fled up the stairs.

"Jasper," she called. His bedroom door was shut. She rapped twice and when no answer came she barged inside.

The window was wide open. The wind blew apart the blue curtains and swept the room. Kelly realized she was shivering.

"Jasper," she said, but he was gone.

She searched the rest of upstairs—the study, her room, the bathroom, the master bedroom—but she knew there was no point. He was gone. How, though? Had he stolen downstairs while she was talking with their father, had he snuck quietly out of the house?

She looked again at the window, touching the rough fabric of the curtains.

Had he gone out the window? She didn't see how that was possible, but she was beginning to realize how some things had a way of proving themselves possible. Had someone—maybe more than one—been waiting for him down below?

She thought back to what had happened in the street and remembered, *Nick.* How could she have forgotten?

She dashed into the hallway and grabbed the phone. "I need to speak to Nick."

The voice that answered was small and young. "Um, is this Kelly?"

"Hi, Sam. Can I speak to Nick?"

"Well," Sam said and again a long pause. She could hear

voices in the background; she thought it might have been their mother and a friend, until the sound of canned laughter made her realize it was a sitcom on TV. "That's kind of the thing—"

"Can you put him on the line?"

"He won't."

"What?"

"He won't come to the phone. He won't touch the phone. He won't move at all. But he keeps saying he needs to speak to *you,* Kelly—he's acting really, really strange and I wish you'd come over—can you please come over?" His young-boy voice seemed to shiver apart and Kelly felt her stomach twist.

"Please," Sam whispered. "Mom and Greg aren't back till later and when they get back—I don't know what they'll do. He's acting like a, like a crazy person. They send crazy people away, don't they? They put them in straitjackets."

"I'm sure it's okay, Sam. It'll be okay. It can't be so bad, at least not—"

"It can," Sam whimpered. "It is that bad, Kelly. Can you come over right now?"

"I'm coming right over."

"Now," Sam said, as if he hadn't heard. "Come now."

As Kelly dropped the phone into the cradle she flashbacked to Archie, kneeling over the unconscious teenager, furling his long thin fingers in Nick's hair and whispering into his ear like the closest of confidants. *Just words,* Kelly thought, *words can't hurt you, change you,* except maybe that was playground wisdom she was learning to outgrow.

She was at the top of the stairs when she heard a car in the driveway. The police were here. As her father's footsteps sounded in the hallway below, Kelly faded back into her bedroom. She couldn't risk questions she didn't know how to answer and she couldn't waste any time; she had to get to Nick.

And Jasper. Somehow I've got to find Jasper.

She went into her room. Unlike Jasper's, her window offered an easy escape route if you were athletic and sure of yourself. She grabbed her red knapsack, took out her textbooks, tossed in a bottle of water and a box of chocolate almonds and her cell phone, and made sure she had some money. Then she paused, scanning the room for anything she could use as some kind of weapon if she absolutely had to. Scissors on the desk. They'd have to do. She tossed them in the knapsack, as well.

Then she was squeezing her long body through the window and stepped from the sill to the lower edge of the roof. She edged along to where the ground below changed from cement porch to soft hilly grass. She grabbed the edge of the roof, swung herself down, hung there a moment, and let herself drop. The fall was longer than she remembered—she hadn't done this in a while—but she bent her knees deeply and landed okay. Her hands were gritty and damp from gripping the roof and she wiped them on her jeans.

No one around front. The officer—assuming there was

only one—had gone inside, and there was nobody in the police car. She wondered if her father was already summoning
her and Jasper, or if he wanted to talk alone with the cop.
Kelly rolled her bike down the driveway, straddled it while it
was moving, and slipped her feet into the pedals. The damp
air poured across her face and through her hair, and she was
free.

CHAPTER FOURTEEN

She coasted down King, trees blurring by on either side. *Somebody is burning leaves,* she thought; she had always liked that smell; but when the hills gave way again to suburbia, the smell struck her as not right, too strong, and then she heard the sound of sirens.

Oh. The word was like a gasp in her mind. *Oh no.*

Archie had said, "I guess we can burn things."

A dark cloud of smoke was drifting out over downtown, bilious shadows twisting against blue sky.

She was on a mission to see Nick. Downtown was out of her way—not by a lot, but her first priority was to see Nick. *If I just drive by really fast,* she thought. *If I just get some idea of what's going on. What's burning.*

She reached the intersection of King and Farris and instead of swinging right and angling down toward Nick's house, she pedaled hard toward downtown. She heard sirens in the air and a helicopter overhead. It was easy to find the fire. It was, she saw with amazement, the big chain bookstore and the little adjoining café; the heat was fierce, shimmering out through the air as flames darted through the upper windows, licked the air, crackled and burned. The air was so sharp it made her eyes water. Kelly hung back, straddling her bike, her vision blocked by the crowd still assembling along the sidewalks. Men were scrambling down from the fire truck, hauling out a hose; someone was screaming something about a cat.

"Is there anyone in there?" Kelly asked the woman standing nearest her. "Is anybody hurt? Did anybody die?"

The woman said, "I think they all got out in time."

"But it's a Saturday," Kelly said. "The place must have been busy."

The man to her right said, "There was a warning. Some kind of phone call."

"A warning," Kelly muttered.

First we burn things. Then we kill things.

People were applauding and cheering. A woman on the sidewalk was holding up a cat, who looked somewhat flattened and very unhappy but otherwise alive and well.

She stayed longer than she'd intended. The spectacle was like an invisible hand holding her in place, there on the sidewalk on her bike. Water snaked through the air; there was a deep rumbling sound, like a train passing by underground, and someone shrieked as part of the roof of the café caved in. "Get back!" someone was yelling. "Get back!" The words broke Kelly's trance as if they'd been personally directed at her; she turned her bike around and pumped the pedals, heading for the river, for Nick's house.

She was two blocks away from the fire when she noticed a loose crowd of people standing beside a row of parked cars on Stannis Street. As she swept past them, she slowed a little to see what they were looking at. Six cars had their windshields smashed in, a letter spray-painted on each, assembling the cars into a chain, to form a name:

J
A
S
P
E
R

"Kelly!" someone yelled out. She recognized Mrs. Wallace, one of the secretaries from school, standing beside the damaged blue Volvo, her eyes blinking behind her little round glasses as Kelly increased her speed and pretended she hadn't heard.

She passed the strip mall and cut through one of the student ghettos—a street of crumbling Victorian houses rented out to students of the local university. Then she was at the river, crossing the bridge, pedaling past the cemetery.

Some of the headstones had been ripped up. She cast them only fleeting glances as she rode past, not wanting to look too closely. But she saw enough: the torn-up grass, the stones broken and upended, the smashed stained-glass windows of the little chapel. Painted across some mossy old stone were the words:

JASPER IT'S TIME

She tore her eyes away and rode faster.

Sam was waiting for her on the porch. He wore baggy jeans and a long-sleeved T-shirt that said "I See Dumb People." When he pushed his bangs from his eyes she saw that they were hazel like Nick's except with a lot more green in them. She wondered if he took flack in the schoolyard for the kind of fine-boned features that many girls would kill for; if he'd developed the swagger and the attitude as a counterpoint.

"Hi," he said. He seemed guarded, as if embarrassed by the way he'd come off on the phone earlier, and determined to prove how tough he really was.

Kelly kicked down the kickstand on her bike and said, "How's Nick?"

"He's . . ." Sam shrugged. "Whatever," he said, shoving his hands in his front pockets, but he couldn't hide the glint of fear in his eyes. "Maybe you can talk some sense into him."

Their house still smelled of paint and sawdust; Nick's uncle was a contractor and Nick had been helping him with a new flurry of renovations. The walls were painted bold, deep colors: red in the hallway, giving way to a deep blue in the living room. "Your bro's on TV," Sam said.

"What?"

Sam picked up the remote control from the couch and aimed it at the television. The local news came on. A pretty blonde reporter stood in front of a crowd, a fire engine half-visible behind her. "I was just there," Kelly said. "The bookstore and Muggy's café, they're totally on fire."

"That's not the bookstore," Sam said. "That's city hall."

She heard the words without really hearing them.

"No," she said. "That can't be city hall." But she looked closer at the screen, at the building behind the reporter. Most of it was obscured by smoke and flame, or the police, ambulance, and fire trucks, or the large and still-gathering crowd of spectators. But she recognized sections of the stately colonial, place of a half-dozen school field trips over the years, the flags out front and the manicured gardens, everything balanced and symmetrical and just so. Now burning.

She felt her whole body go funny. She braced herself against the back of the couch. Sam turned up the volume. The reporter was saying, ". . . stunning developments this Saturday afternoon as a series of fires sweep through this peaceful and idyllic town . . ."

"There's this other fire going on in the warehouse district," Sam said, "but I think they managed to put that one out before it got too bad."

"They're really . . ." She had to go around and sit on the couch. She doubled over and took deep breaths. "They're burning down the town. How many people have died?"

"They were saying no one. So far."

She lifted her head. "No one."

"They got warnings—wait, she's talking about it now."

". . . amazingly, no deaths or serious injuries so far. Details are unclear, but witnesses are saying that in each case people were warned beforehand through phone calls to get out of the buildings, and that several individuals actually assisted people in doing just this. However, these same individuals spread the word that soon there will be no more warnings and no more assistance, that events will become, quote, more baffling and more tragic, unquote. Anyone with any information about these individuals—"

"It's that guy in the road," Sam said. "The guy who hurt Nick. Does he have evil superpowers or something?"

Kelly swallowed. Her throat was so dry. "Something like that," she muttered and pressed her hands together. A very cold, breathless feeling was stealing through her.

"It's Jasper," Nick said suddenly. "Wait, see, he's on again," and pointed at the television.

A photograph of Jasper, taken from the high school yearbook, filled the screen. The blonde reporter was saying, "Jasper Ruland is wanted for questioning in what appears to be the most staggering and bewildering case of arson this city has ever seen—although he is not necessarily a suspect, at least not yet, repeated mentions and appearances of his name appear to indicate some kind of connection—"

"Did Jasper start the fires?" Sam looked bewildered.

"No. Of course not."

"That's what I thought. It's the strange people in the road?"

"Yes."

"Why are they writing Jasper's name everywhere?"

They're turning the town against him. They want him to know this isn't his home anymore.

"—anyone who knows this teenager's whereabouts, please call—"

Kelly grabbed the remote from the boy and clicked off the TV.

The silence was a relief.

Half-hidden by the thatch of bangs, Sam's eyes looked wide and unhappy.

"You have to fix Nick," he said quietly. "Whatever this dude Archie's done, or your brother's done—you know what it is, right? You can fix it before our parents come home?"

"I'll try."

"Fix it," Sam ordered, "or else they'll send him away to the nuthouse and pump him full of drugs."

She went up the steps, the wooden banister trembling a bit in her hand. The upstairs hallway was just a stub, Nick's bedroom off to the right. She rapped on the door. "Nick?"

A muttered response from within.

She pushed open the door.

At first glance she thought the room was empty. It was small, sparse, neat: a twin bed with a wooden headboard, a wooden dresser, a desk in the corner, a bulletin board tacked with postcard reproductions of photographs and paintings Nick liked, some of which they'd collected together when they'd gone into the city to the MoMA and the Met. Unlike the vividly painted walls of the rest of the house, the walls in here were cream-colored, the throw on the bed a patchwork of desert shades. There was an old football on the bookshelf. Nick didn't play the game or watch it all that much, but she knew the football had something to do with his dad. He didn't keep any photographs of his father—at least not any that Kelly had seen—and never talked about him at all, just kept that football perched on the bookshelf, gathering dust.

A voice croaked, "About time."

Nick was curled on the floor in the corner, squeezed into the narrow space between the wall and the bed. One side of his face was bruised and swollen. She remembered again the sick sound of impact when Archie's fist had flown at his face. "Serves us right," Nick muttered. "We believed it. We all bought into it."

"Bought into what?"

"The lie."

"What lie?"

"Is it a lie when you change reality?" His voice assumed a musing tone. "Because it's different, yeah, it's not what it's supposed to be. It's false. So yeah. It's a lying reality. But I had that feeling and I didn't listen to it. You didn't really listen to it, either. Convinced yourself you were going crazy, you know? So we weren't paying attention to the wrongness. We didn't look close enough."

"Nick." Her voice was just a whisper, although she didn't mean it to be. She couldn't seem to make it any stronger.

"Four thirty-two," Nick said. "Four thirty-two. That's the number on the door."

The number sounded familiar. "What door?"

"The door you need to go through."

"Nick. You don't sound like yourself."

"No," Nick agreed. "But we still need to talk."

She sat on the edge of the bed. Waited.

"I saw," Nick said. "For just a moment. I saw. When he tasted my soul and decided he didn't want it. He didn't want it. It's not good enough for Archie." He gave her a thin-lipped smile that sent a shudder down her spine. "Not like your brother's," he said. "Your brother's soul is like crack to him. He'll do anything to get it."

She reached out to touch him, but he recoiled.

"No," he said. "No touching. I'm alone, you see."

"You're not alone."

"Alone in here." Nick tapped his temple. "Except we all are, aren't we? Archie knows. He *knows*. 'All alone, I beweep my outcast state.'"

"What did Archie tell you?"

"He showed me what he is."

"What is he?"

"The exile," Nick said. "The outcast. The stranger. That's what he is. That's why he needs his boys. To keep him company. Their souls keep him cozy. That's why he collects them. Those souls. They make him feel he's got one of his own."

Nick pressed his hands together, muttering to himself. She couldn't hear what he was saying, wasn't sure she wanted to try. *Sam is right,* she thought. *He's broken. Archie broke him.*

"Nick," she said and paused, fighting down a rising sense of panic. "You're scaring Sam. Tell you the truth, you're scaring me."

"How long? How long?" Nick tipped his head back and laughed. "Don't be scared, Kelly. You have to be brave, Kelly, or else we're lost. Jasper. Me. And you, too, probably. Archie knows you now. He smells you now. He might go away, in the end, but he'll never let you go." He was twisting his fingers together. "He's waiting for you," Nick said. "That's what I'm supposed to tell you. He's waiting for you, so you'd better go. Or people start to die."

"I don't know what to do," Kelly whispered.

Nick leaned forward and dropped his voice to a whisper. "You can change it back, Kelly. See, this is what he doesn't know I saw. But I saw it. What he took, what he changed, you can change it back. Because it's all about you. Do you understand? You can take the lie and turn it back into truth."

"I don't understand. I don't understand."

"It's the bargain Jasper made." Nick's voice was a hiss.

She was shaking her head. He was leading her to a place where she could not go, would not go, because that shadow-coffin feeling was hovering over her again. *The void,* she thought.

"Can't you feel it?" Nick was saying. "The wrongness. It's been in the air ever since that night. That night we hooked up at the rave—"

"But I wasn't there. I couldn't go. I was grounded!"

"—some of that lie, you can fix. You can. But it has to be you. It can't be anyone else, not for this. And that's why you have to go to him. Not for his reasons. For your reasons. So you can make it true again."

"I wasn't there that night," Kelly said. "I wasn't. I was

grounded. I was watching *Buffy the Vampire Slayer* on DVD—"

Nick put his head in his hands.

She reached out to touch his shoulder but again he recoiled.

"You need to be in the hospital," she said. "Your head."

"Doctors can't fix me," Nick said. "Can't fix Jasper. It's all up to you. So be a big girl. Deal with it. Deal with *all* of it."

"But I don't know what to do!"

"Don't say that," Nick whispered, "because it's not true. Here." His hand slipped beneath the bed and she heard a small jangling sound. He lifted something out and handed it toward her: keys on an army knife keychain.

"Here," Nick said again. "You can take Truck."

When she was at the bedroom doorway, he called out again: "Remember what he is," he said. "See through him, and you can defeat him."

"What is he, then? What is Archie?"

"Nothing," Nick said, and laughed.

CHAPTER FIFTEEN

What am I doing, she thought.

She hadn't allowed herself to think too much about it. She hadn't allowed herself to think at all. Sam had been waiting at the foot of the creaky little staircase when she came out of Nick's room. Before he could finish opening his mouth to speak, she barked, "Call nine-one-one. Get him to a hospital. Now."

Sam said, "But—"

"I'm going to try to fix him, Sam. I'm going to do all I can. Okay?"

Sam followed her out onto the porch. "But that's Nick's truck."

The driver's door tended to stick and she had to yank extra hard to make it open. "I'm borrowing it."

"Are you going to go see this Archie dude?"

She looked at him over the top of the door. "Yeah," she said, tossing her red knapsack in the backseat. She slipped in behind the wheel. She didn't have a license yet, only a learner's permit. It was going to have to do.

Sam looked on from the porch, his dark hair in his eyes.

Where the hell did she think she was going?

Except Nick was right. She'd known all along.

The Heath house.

From what Kelly had gleaned from books and movies, every town had a place like the Heath house, a house that seemed to fall outside mundane day-to-day reality, that became the subject of rumors and stories and dares. For the longest time, the hilltop property had been abandoned, ever since a family—or so it was rumored—packed up and left in the middle of the night. Kelly's mother said the real reason had to do with domestic violence—the wife finally snapped, collected kids and dog, and took off and the husband moved into the city—but the rumors she'd heard growing up involved the corpses of animals and secret rituals. Another story had the family on the run from the mob.

Eventually someone bought the property, knocked down the house—a bland ranchhouse from the fifties—and tried to build one of those tacky McMansions that were sprouting in the hillsides. A construction worker fell to his death and stories about the property's bad vibes began circulating all over again. The owner lost all his money and the project was abandoned. The goth kids at school adopted the house as a special interest of theirs, went on about spells and rituals and paranormal forces and were rumored to sneak onto the property at night to play vampire games.

Finally the property once again changed hands and the half-completed megamonstrosity was torn down. The new owners were a wealthy couple from New York who'd brought in a famous architect—although Kelly could never remember his name—to design and build the place for them, a sprawling poured-concrete structure that Kelly's mother called *postmodern* and other people called *damn ugly*. It took almost two years for the house to get finished—and then no one moved in. The place stood empty. Kelly knew from her father, whose restaurant was the only place in town where the famous architect would deign to eat, that the couple had decided to divorce and were fighting over who got the kids, the lion's share of the art collection, and the Selridge house. When the subject came up at school, Kelly was quick to explain this, but kids would only talk over her. "Evil," they said. "The place is evil. No one can live there."

She was cresting the first hill when something came flying out of the darkness and slammed against her windshield. For a moment she saw it: a face. Distorted, leering, grotesque. Sliding down her windshield like a dead bird. Kelly shrieked and the steering wheel seemed to wrench in her hands, taking on a life of its own. She felt Truck swerve, skid; she tapped the brakes; the vehicle came to rest against the guardrail. The thing on the windshield—whatever it had been—was now gone.

She leaned her forehead against the steering wheel. She was trembling. She tried the ignition but the car wouldn't start. She tried again, floored it, but the engine just wouldn't catch. She'd have to walk. She wasn't that far anyway.

Now, as she got out of Truck and slammed the door and stared up at the house through the gathering dark, she remembered what Morgan had said the last time they'd done E: "You know, when we first moved into this stupid McMansion? I didn't want this room, because I didn't like this view. It's like, every time I find myself looking up at that house, I feel like that house is looking back into me. You know?"

The house seemed alive; music pounded down across the hillside and, as she left the road behind her and cut up across the grass, she smelled woodsmoke. Her mind flashed to the fires burning downtown. As she crested the hill and looked across the property, she saw a series of fires burning in steel drums, staggered across the grass. The shadowy shapes of Riders drifted through the flickering light thrown off by the flames and she heard, through the heavy bass of music, the sounds of conversation and laughter. The house itself rose up beyond, the windows like bright, blind eyes . . . The shapes of motorcycles loomed like tombstones across the property and along the road.

. . . and then the house seemed to change, to shift.

She wrinkled her forehead. She wasn't sure exactly what she'd seen, only—there—it seemed to happen again—the windows looked to be in slightly different places and hadn't the roof been flat, before? Now it lifted into a peak. Walking toward the house, she kept staring at it, and it seemed as if the surrounding air was shimmering. As if the house seemed to occupy a different kind of space than everything and everyone around it.

She remembered something else from that night at Morgan's house, only this time they'd been words of her own:

"Doesn't it seem weird? . . . It's like the house isn't staying completely still."

But then a Rider was stepping—although he moved with such grace he didn't seem to walk so much as flow—into the space in front of her.

It was the dark-haired Rider in the torn blue leathers.

"Your friend," he said. His voice was a rasp. "How's your friend?"

"Excuse me," Kelly muttered, trying not to let on just how nervous she was, attempting to step around him. But he moved as she moved. He seemed to grow taller every moment, his soulless eyes gazing down on her, his lips twisted in that strange little smile. And even though *cold* doesn't really have a smell . . . that's how he smelled to her. Like the white silent cold of deep winter. His skin, this close, had a faint blue tinge; but the light in his eyes burned fiercely.

"You're the reason," he said.

"What—what reason?"

"You're the reason we're here. Still here. In this stinking town."

"What—"

"That's her," someone else said. "Look. It's her."

Another voice: "That's the sister."

And then the voices were all overlapping: "The sister?"

"Over there . . ."

"She owes us, the stupid bitch—"

Riders were falling in all around them. How many of them were there? They seemed endless. For every face she now recognized, knew she'd glimpsed before, she saw two or three more that she didn't.

The Rider who stood in front of her said, "You think we're here in this little shit town 'cause we *want* to be? Riders need to *ride*, little girl. Riders need to be on the *road*. On the *move*."

"Then go." She tried to duck around him, but no matter how fast she was—or thought she was—he was faster, even though he didn't seem to move at all.

"Being cooped up in one place like this? You know what's it like? Feels like? Torture. All because of you. You're the reason."

Something hit her on the cheek, fell to her feet. A stone. She looked around in surprise. Another stone came darting through the firelight and she moved aside but felt it graze her shoulder, harder than the first. "Hey," she yelled, but another stone struck her right temple. Her arms came up around her head. She heard laughter.

"Was up to me," growled the Rider in front of her, "I would have just killed you and your brother both. Never got what the whole fuss is about."

"Let her through."

A man stood on the roof of the Heath house, silhouetted against the last of the setting sun. His voice flowed both over and under the music, rolled across them all, and people were quick to pay attention: breaking off their own conversations, turning away from one another, toward him. Toward Archie.

"Let her through," he said again. "Anyone who touches her gets their hand cut off."

The Rider who had been right in her face took three large steps away from her.

Someone turned off the music.

Silence smashed down on them. Then came the rustling sounds of movement as people began to fall away from her on either side. Gripping the strap of her knapsack so tightly that her knuckles ached, Kelly put one foot in front of the other. It was too unnerving to look around her—at the unnatural faces of the Riders—so Kelly kept her head down, studying the toes of her sneakers sticking out from the frayed hems of her jeans as they moved one in front of each other and carried her across the cold dead grass.

Then she was at the house, stone steps leading up to an iron-studded wooden door that looked as if it properly belonged on a fortress somewhere. It was shut and locked.

She looked up at the roof, squinting into the glare of sunset, but the man had disappeared. When she dropped her gaze, the iron-studded door now yawned wide open. Beyond it she saw only shadow. *The door is like a mouth,* she couldn't help thinking, and the house like some weird living thing that wanted to eat her.

They're burning things, she told herself. *They're killing things. They won't stop till they get my brother.*

Telling herself this helped her go up those stone steps and inside the house.

CHAPTER SIXTEEN

Hallways and more hallways.
　No doors. No windows.
No rooms.
Just hallways.

Faded brown carpet covered the floor. Paint flaked off the walls and the air smelled of mold and decay. The walls were scrawled with graffiti, but it was unlike any graffiti Kelly had ever seen before:

> FLESH PERISHES
> I LIVE ON—PROJECTING TRAIT AND
> 　TRACE—
> THROUGH TIMES TO TIMES ANON—
> AND LEAPING FROM PLACE TO PLACE—
> 　OVER OBLIVION

Strange shadows flickered at the end of the hallway and as she drew closer, she heard voices, music, laughter. But all she saw was a wall and more decrepit hallway stretching to her left and right. Still, she heard the voices and the music, as if a party was going on right alongside her.

In another dimension, maybe. Another reality. Echoing down to me in this one.

She no longer knew how long she'd been wandering through this weird never-ending maze of a house, but she was seized by the unnerving feeling that she was going to be doing this forever. The house was a trap and she'd fallen right into it. She felt a fluttering inside her stomach, then the fluttering became faster and harder and reached up into her chest. "Stop," she told herself. And still that laughter echoed in the air, the voices layered in multiple conversations, the backbeat of music: somewhere there was a party going on, excitement and glamour, but she was doomed to wander, forever stuck, in these dingy depressing hallways—

"Stop," she said again. Her voice seemed very loud and very strange in the hallway. She obeyed her own command: dropping her knapsack and sitting on the floor, hugging her knees to her chest.

Be calm. Think this through.

This house, this space . . . this is a weird place. The rules are different here. Maybe there are no rules.

But as she thought this, the fluttering in her stomach only worsened and she felt herself breathing high and fast. What had she been thinking, to come here in the first place? *Jasper needs me. I have to turn the lie into truth, whatever that means.* But she was just a teenage girl, all alone, against Archie and his minions—

Am I really all alone?

I have at least one friend. Don't I?

Someone who wants to help me?

She looked in both directions, gazing down the bleak reaches of hallway. "Coyote," she whispered. "Coyote. Come help me."

Nothing happened.

"Coyote," she said again.

And when nothing continued to happen, she felt more foolish than ever.

Think this through. There's got to be something I'm missing.

Her mind worked back through the things Nick had told her, Jasper had told her. Nothing seemed helpful. And then:

The truth is behind and between things.

Who had said that?

So you must always look beneath the surface. Always, always, always.

Archie had said that, she realized, the first time she'd encountered him in the classroom, when he'd made her believe he was a teacher named Mr. Archer.

So maybe she wasn't looking closely enough. Maybe there was an answer right in front of her . . .

Kelly stared at the wall.

. . . *literally* right in front of her.

Now that she was staring directly at it, the wall didn't seem very . . . solid. It had an odd, airy shimmer to it, like a projection. She touched the wall, flattened her hand against it. It seemed solid enough and she couldn't help but feel a throb of disappointment . . . except then she felt the material shiver beneath her fingers, felt it begin to shift and change—

On impulse she hurled herself against it.

And felt herself slipping through it.

She was in yet another hallway, but at least it was one she hadn't been in before. The light flickered, then went very dim. She saw motion at the end of the hall. Someone was down there. "Hello?" she called out, but the figure didn't answer.

She looked behind her, but the space had dropped away into darkness. It was like gazing at a wall of black. *Keep away,* an inner voice told her. She had the sudden feeling that if she stepped into all that shadow, the floor beneath her would dissolve . . . and she would fall into the abyss. She would fall and fall.

Nowhere to go but forward.

Toward that figure waiting for her at the end of the hall.

"Hello?" she called out, her voice soft, but there was no response. As she drew closer, she saw that the figure was clearly female, tall and young with brown hair that fell past her shoulders, dressed in jeans and a black leather jacket . . . The figure was her. She was walking straight toward her own life-size reflection in a gilded mirror.

"Hello," her reflection called out, soft, just the way Kelly had moments before. "Hello."

"What's happening?" Kelly said.

Her reflection said, "What's happening?"

And then, even as Kelly stood there completely motionless, the Kelly girl in the mirror reached out and placed the palms of her hands flat against the glass. Kelly stared at those palms for a moment before she noticed. There were no lines in the skin. No life line, no heart line, none of those things Kelly remembered from when she and Amy had studied a book about palm reading.

Kelly lifted her gaze from the mirror girl's hands and saw that the mirror girl was staring right back at her. The mirror girl's mouth twisted into a smirk.

"Who are you?" Kelly said.

"Who are you?" the girl echoed, but her tone was different this time, not merely copying Kelly's but shading into mockery. Then she said, "Want to come inside?"

"Is my brother in there?"

"What do you think?"

Kelly looked behind her.

That solid-seeming wall of darkness was moving down the corridor, eating up the air, closing the distance between it and her. Jasper's words came back to her: "You have to be able to look straight into the abyss. You have to have the mental strength . . . or else it eats you alive."

She turned and confronted the darkness. Tunneling toward her, killing off escape routes. She had nowhere to go.

But what if that wasn't the abyss?

She turned back to the mirror. The girl in the mirror. The girl's outstretched palms, wiped clean of all marks of identity. "Come inside," the girl whispered.

Kelly touched her own palms to the glass.

The other Kelly's hands darted out through the glass and clamped around Kelly's wrists, her touch so cold Kelly felt it to the bone. She sucked in breath. And felt herself pulled against mirror, then through it, and she was pitching forward into a whole new kind of space.

CHAPTER SEVENTEEN

She was standing in a library.

It wasn't like any library she had ever been in before; it was more like some Hollywood idea of what a library should be: grand, magnificent, larger than life. The white marble ceiling seemed to lift itself higher and higher even as Kelly watched. The walls were lined with gleaming oak bookcases filled with books. Even the fire in the fireplace seemed too hot, too bright, like a small sun inside borders of stone.

A small round shape drifted off the edge of her vision. She turned. A glass sphere about the size of a baseball hung in the air. It dangled there, as if on an unseen string, before beginning to move again. It was rising, and as Kelly's gaze followed it up, she saw at least a hundred more spheres suspended in the air like wind chimes, except they moved without benefit of wind, and they moved in a deliberate pattern, crisscrossing through the air, weaving around and through one another as if in a choreographed ballet.

"Isn't it a stunning collection?" said a voice from behind her. "Doesn't it *blow you away?*"

Archie was standing in front of the fireplace. A Rider in black leather stood just behind him, his hands clasped and his head bowed. Kelly glanced quickly at the Rider, thought, *No, that can't be him,* and refused to look again. Archie wore narrow lace-up trousers, a faded denim shirt, his white-blond hair brushed back from his high forehead. His eyes were as bright as the flames and just as intense. His skin was so smooth, so unlined . . . she didn't remember him seeming so young before. Dressed like that, leaning against the stone wall and tossing an apple from hand to hand, he could have been an unusually beautiful college student.

He said, "You could just stand there and look at them all day, couldn't you?" He tossed the apple high in the air, caught it, laughed. He seemed in a very good mood. "Some days I do exactly that."

"What are they?"

"Souls," he said and seemed surprised that she had bothered to ask. "Each of those spheres contains one soul." He bit into an apple with a loud moist crunch, then gestured to a tray that had suddenly appeared on the mantel. Green apples were stacked in a little pyramid. "Take one," he said. "They're very good."

"No thanks."

"Wise," he said and nodded approvingly. "When you find yourself in a strange, enchanted land, never accept anything to eat or drink. Or else you'll be trapped there forever."

"I didn't realize."

"You learn something new every day."

"Is this what this place is? Some kind of . . . enchanted land?"

"This is the room of souls." Archie bit into the apple again.

"The room of souls," she echoed.

"Your brother's soul is in one of those things. When it comes around this way I'll point it out to you."

She was so dazzled by the glimmering procession of the spheres, the patterns they slowly wove through the air, that it took several moments for the true meaning of them to hit her. Those spheres were cages. Nothing more.

Soul cages.

All their beauty fell away. She scowled, refused to look at them again.

"Don't be like that," Archie chided. "I *earned* those souls. Each and every one of them." He rubbed his hands together, then held them out toward the fireplace. "This damn realm of yours," he muttered. "Never warm enough."

Kelly's voice turned very soft. "So what exactly are you?"

He shrugged, as if the question didn't much interest him. "An exile."

"No, I mean . . . what are you?"

He shrugged again. And again, she was struck by how young he seemed. "I have no memory," Archie said. "Which means I have no past. Both these things—my memory, my past—were taken from me, gone from me, when I woke up in this realm. This crappy dinky realm that includes your world and a few others that aren't half as interesting. So I am an exile through and through. If we are what we remember, if we are the place we came from, if we are what we're attached to, then I am nothing. You understand?"

Nothing. What Nick had said.

"You're attached to those souls," Kelly said. "In their little glass cages."

"True. A paradox, those spheres. So strong. Yet so fragile."

"And beautiful."

"Yes."

"Is that what makes you choose a soul? Beauty?"

"Don't be simple. Even the most twisted little soul has beauty and charm." He tilted back his head, as if in thought. *He's enjoying this,* Kelly realized, as if he didn't get the chance to discuss this very often. He continued, "All souls are beautiful, and *so* delicious to taste, but only a few of them *compel* me. *Pull* me. Because only a few souls seem . . . *familiar* in some way." He nodded, looked pleased with the word.

"Familiar," Kelly said.

"There's something about them that reminds me of myself," he said. "I mean—not as I am now, forever the *exile,* the *stranger*—but as I was. Once upon a time. When I was still . . . unfallen."

"So it's your way of trying to find yourself." Kelly spoke slowly, trying to put this in a way that made sense to her. "Trying to find a way back to who and what you used to be."

"Look at you." His tone was affectionate. "Playing psychologist."

She was trying to figure out what resemblance to himself he could possibly find in someone like her brother. But then her eyes went again to the books—the books on books on books, forming a ladder of books as far up as her eye could see—and she thought of the fragments of poetry he seemed to like to quote. That love for the written word, that hunger for books, for knowledge. Jasper had always had that, ever since he learned to read at three years old, and it had always held him apart from the other kids, who would accuse him of thinking too much or using too many big words. Maybe Archie was drawn to the streak of outsider that ran all through Jasper, even when he'd learned to hide it, even when he had been at his most popular. *I all alone beweep my outcast state.* She had thought that Archie had been sending a message to Jasper about who and what he'd become since the car accident; now she saw that Archie might have simply been describing himself. Or both of them. Maybe Archie collected those souls—consumed those souls—because he just figured they belonged to him in the first place.

Kelly said, "Can I see your wings?"

Archie lifted pale eyebrows.

She was trying to find some way to stall him, but her request held sincerity. "I saw them . . . that night in the mist, and . . . and I wanted . . ."

"I don't see why not," Archie decided and in one fluid sweeping motion slipped off the denim shirt. His torso was smooth, neatly chiseled, perfectly hairless; the skin didn't seem like skin at all, but living marble that rose and fell with his breathing yet seemed too cold to touch. He turned his back to her. She saw with a jolt that there was nothing human about his back. It was draped with something soft, and midnight blue, and alive, something that started to twitch and ripple. His wings: folded so intricately and laid so flat across his body that they were like a second skin, perfectly concealed by regular clothing.

The wings lifted themselves away from Archie and began to unfurl. They moved upward and outward with such grace they were like rivers rippling out through the air. He turned back toward her to face her, white-blond alabaster man with laser-bright eyes and wings like deep night.

She couldn't speak.

He grinned. He swept the air with his wings, still grinning, creating pulses of wind that ran through her hair and tugged at her clothes. It was both pleasant and repulsive at the same time: she felt as if Archie was touching her. She saw how he was heightening the drama, the spectacle, of himself. He was enjoying her attention. He was showing off.

He stretched out his wings to their full extent—they had a span, Kelly gauged, of at least eight feet, and even while he stood completely still the wings seemed to shimmer, to move, different angles and edges winking in and out of her vision, and it occurred to her that maybe, like this house, like Archie himself, they could not be contained in just one dimension.

Then Archie folded himself up. The wings slipped in on themselves, collapsing neatly down behind his body until they disappeared from view. Archie seemed a young man again, if paler and stranger than most.

And now that the wings had been taken away from her, Kelly could turn and look at the Rider behind him.

"Jasper," she said.

"Go home, Kelly," he said quietly. "It's over. It's done."

"But it can't be." Her voice trembled, broke. "It can't be."

"I made a huge mistake coming back," Jasper said. "But I think I fixed it in time. Before something really horrible could happen."

"But something horrible is happening now."

"You know, I'm glad you dropped by," Archie said. "The original plan was to hold you hostage, have your little friend Nick fill your head with delusions of rescue so you would scurry over here. 'He that hath a wife and children hath given hostages to fortune,' as Francis Bacon said. Do you know who Francis Bacon is?"

"No."

"I'm sure one day you will. Interesting lad, Bacon was. I knew him very briefly. His soul had a vinegary cast to it . . ." For a moment he seemed to drift into reverie. "I foresaw some negotiation, a bit of threatening, all of that. Annoying. But Jasper decided to save us the bother." Archie beamed at his Rider. "Kelly. You're free to go. Have the *nicest* of lives."

He made a quick gesture to his right, and a door appeared where just moments before there had only been air. "Step through that and you'll be back where you belong with your lovely parents. They're starting to wonder where you are, you realize."

Kelly whispered, "Only if Jasper comes with me."

"Oh, *please*," Archie said. " Please! Quit making my life so difficult! I am so tired of this . . . I changed *reality* for you people and this is how you thank me?"

Jasper said nothing. Kelly kept glancing from one to the other. *Archie looks so young,* she thought, *and Jasper so old;* as if Archie was draining and drinking Jasper's life force. *He's like a kind of vampire,* Kelly thought. *A soul-sucking vampire.*

Archie stood with his head lowered. Kelly could hear her heartbeat in her ears, hammering out the moments. When Archie looked at them again, his eyes were black fire.

"I changed *reality* for you," he said again. "Do you know how complicated that is? To go in and out of parallel universes, take a piece from here, a piece from there, switch them around, line everything up so there aren't too many shockwaves screwing up the cosmos? Do you know how *stressful* that is? I get *headaches*." The finger he was pointing at her brother seemed to lengthen even as Kelly watched. Then Archie sighed and folded his hands in the pockets of his military-style coat that Kelly didn't remember him wearing just moments before.

Archie took a long breath, held it for a moment, then let it out slowly.

He smiled at Kelly.

"Look," he said. "You'll be fine. As soon as you step through that door you'll forget your brother even existed."

"No. Never happen. Impossible."

"And yet," Archie said gently, "it's true. You will forget about him. Everybody will forget about him. That's part of what it means to lose your soul."

"Go, Kelly," Jasper, or the Rider who had once been Jasper, said quietly. "It's done. There's nothing you can do. Go home and get on with your life."

Kelly looked at the door that signaled freedom, tried to imagine stepping into a place where she had no brother. Imagined sitting with her parents in, say, a roadside café maybe six months or two years or ten years from now and the sudden thunder of motorcycles would make them turn their heads; imagined watching lean ragged figures rolling up in front of the café, turning off their engines and kicking down the kickstands and swinging their legs off the bikes; imagined one boy catching their attention, because he seemed familiar somehow, even though they were sure they had never seen him before, but there was something in the shape of the jaw, the cheekbones, the lanky build, that reminded them rather vaguely of themselves; imagined locking gazes with this person through the café window, and seeing a deadness, a hollowness in those eyes, as if the person before her wasn't a young man but a wraith. A living wraith. Imagined how she would turn away, relief juddering through her so strong it was like sickness, because she would be thinking, *Of course we don't know him. How could we know a person like that?*

Never knowing. Never suspecting.

Now, standing in the library as the flames sputtered,

Kelly realized she couldn't stop shaking her head. "I can't," she said. "I won't."

But Archie wasn't listening. "*There* it is," he said. "Let me show this to you before you go, sweet thing. I think you'll appreciate it."

He tilted his head back, studied the shifting arrangement of glass spheres in the air above them, as they crisscrossed one another and wove through one another. "That one," Archie said.

He lifted a hand and made a beckoning motion.

One of the spheres drifted downward, angling through the air toward Archie's outstretched hand. "Now," Archie said, and his voice filled with a warm buttery tone of relief, "finally. Mine."

Kelly didn't respond.

She couldn't.

Because in the space behind Archie sat the coyote.

The coyote tilted his head at her, gold-green eyes softly glowing. He wanted her to be quiet, Kelly knew, not to give his presence away. She looked over at Archie, who seemed too intent on the sphere to notice anything or anyone else in the room. "Oh," Archie muttered, "it seems we didn't quite . . . *finish.*" Archie muttered beneath his breath and as Kelly watched, a wispy gleaming vapor began to slip out of Jasper's mouth, Jasper's eyes and nostrils. Archie spoke a few words—Kelly didn't recognize the language, suspected it was no language from this world—and the vapor curled like a snake around the glass sphere and then began to penetrate the glass, to fill the space inside.

What happened next happened very quickly.

The air blurred with motion. Something flew through the air and knocked the glass sphere from Archie's hand. Archie cried out and Jasper stared with a dulled, vacant gaze—a soulless gaze—as the sphere hit the rug with a muffled cracking sound and a shaggy tan-and-black shape hit the floor after it. "You," Archie yelled. Kelly thought he meant her, but then realized he was looking at the coyote. "I knew you were behind this. Look, I'm sorry, okay? I was in a bad mood that day. Give me—" The coyote scooped the ball between his jaws and in a single leaping bound closed the space between himself and Kelly. She felt a cool damp nose thrust itself into her hand, felt warm breath, the edge of teeth; and then the coyote was leaping away from her and she had the glass sphere in her hand.

Thin cracks had spiderwebbed all along its surface; the vapor inside was rippling and moving as if it was a live thing, and agitated.

"THAT IS MINE," a voice screamed and a wind blasted through the room, whipping up the flames in the fireplace and flinging back Kelly's hair, "THAT IS MINE, STUPID GIRL, GIVE IT TO ME—"

There was a man coming at her, his body rising up and twisting toward her, a man who was not a man but something else, with spitting red eyes and rows on rows of teeth, chomping through the air for her face—

Kelly dropped the ball and reared back her foot. She was back on the soccer field, her team looking to her to make the winning goal. She kicked.

It flew at the fireplace.

And then came a sound of shattering glass that was so loud and went on for so long that it became a kind of music. Archie's body bent completely backward. He was howling. The howling filled the air, the shards of glass danced through it, as Kelly tightened both hands on her knapsack.

And then she didn't know where she was.

CHAPTER EIGHTEEN

The white light was so complete, so dazzling, so blinding, she couldn't tell if she was alone or not; she listened for any signs of breathing, movement, rustling of clothing, anything to indicate that either her brother or Archie was nearby. "Jasper?" she called.

Nothing.

Only silence.

But then she felt a warm tongue lick her fingers.

A voice said, *Just us.*

She said, aware that she was both frowning and breathless, "Coyote?"

Me.

A cool damp nose touched her palm; she closed her fingers gently around shaggy fur, the tip of an ear.

"I can't believe this is happening."

The animal chuffed warm breath against her wrist. *You and me both.*

"Where are we?"

This is—Coyote paused, and Kelly realized that the animal had a sense of the dramatic,—*this is Jasper's dark night of the soul.*

"But this isn't night."

True. It's more of a metaphor. She heard a rustle of movement, a scratching, heard the ruffle of fur as the animal shook himself out. *Everyone has one. It's an actual time and place and we're standing in the thick of it. This is what Archie keeps bottled up. This is his prize. The moment that he claims as his, that he takes and changes.* Again, the dramatic pause. *This is your chance to get it back. To set it right. Because some bargains should not be kept, yes? They are not fair. Young ones like your brother never get . . . all the information. A tricky, tricky one is Archie.*

"I have the power to change it?"

You think I'd bring you here for nothing?

"Why are you doing this?"

A sigh. *Archie and I go way back. But this thing that he does with the souls, with the young ones: I do not approve of this. I spoke to him of this. He did not take it well.*

"What did he do to you?"

Drugged me and sold me to a truly wretched human who—But no. Let's not, as you say, go there.

"You're doing this for revenge against Archie?"

Perhaps that. Perhaps I am in debt to your brother, yes? Perhaps I am amusing myself. One must keep oneself amused, after all.

"Where do you come from?"

Not here.

"Another—another world, or something? Another reality?"

More like an overlooked corner of this one.

"And Archie?"

Ah, Archie. The mystery of Archie. I hear rumors, among our kind—

"Your kind. Other—other talking animals?"

The coyote cast her a look. *We are outsiders and watchers. We bear witness. We keep the stories. We pass the stories on.*

"I thought you were some kind of trickster," Kelly said.

We meddle if we feel we must, to keep the story interesting.

"What's the story on Archie?"

As I said. Rumors only. He committed a great crime, in his home realm, and was forever exiled. He found himself here. His brother followed, out of love and concern for him, but they also had a falling-out. Archie does not take criticism well.

"People with big egos and secret insecurities tend not to," Kelly said. "My mother told me that. I think she might have been talking about my father at the time, although—"

The white light began to dim a little. Kelly felt firm ground beneath her feet. Familiar shapes resolved themselves around her: houses, a sidewalk, streetlights softly glowing. "This is my street," she said. "We're standing in front of my house."

Coyote was sitting beside her. He brushed a paw against his nose and said, *Look.*

A girl was climbing out of a window. Kelly realized with

a sharp jolt that it was her bedroom window, that the girl was . . . her. She watched as the girl gripped the bottom edge of the windowsill and let herself hang, a shadowy figure against the brick. She swung herself out and dropped into soft grass. She disappeared around the back of the house and then came around the other side, wheeling her bike down the driveway.

She can't see you, Coyote said, as the girl pedaled down the street. There was a moment when Kelly could have reached out and touched her, she passed by so close.

Kelly said, "Have we gone back in time?"

We've gone into the night that Archie suspended in his little cage. This is the night that Archie changed. This is your chance to change it back. You do that, you change everything, and your brother will be free.

"This is the night of the rave," Kelly said. "This is the night I was grounded."

Grounded. But it would appear you're sneaking out, yes?

"Where am I going?"

Think hard. The memory is there.

Kelly felt warm wind against her face. She said, "I'm going to Nick's house."

You're going to split into two versions of yourself, the coyote warned. *Part of you will stay here, with me, watching things unfold. And the other part of you is going to go back into the person who you were all those months ago, the person you just saw sneaking out of her bedroom window.*

"But how—" Kelly was about to say, when those words were taken from her.

Because suddenly she was on Nick's doorstep and she had time to think, *I'm that girl again,* and, *Something is going to happen tonight, something bad,* but then the door opened and Nick, a slightly younger, thinner Nick with longer hair, was there in front of her and all such thoughts flew from her mind. "Hi," Kelly heard herself say. "Are you ready to go?"

CHAPTER NINETEEN

He was in jeans, a blue hooded sweatshirt, and seemed surprised to see her. "Hi."

Kelly grinned at him. "Let's go," she said. "Are you ready?"

He was about to answer when a slightly overeager voice called out from behind him, "Nick? Who's that?"

Nick rolled his eyes and muttered, "C'mon." She followed him through the hallway and down the steps into a family room. The walls were a burnt orange; pottery and colorful glassware were displayed on the shelves. Magazines and newspapers and books were strewn everywhere. A bowl of half-eaten popcorn was on the coffee table. An opened laptop sat beside it. His mother, she knew, was a social worker who wrote paranormal romance novels on the side. A woman in a sweeping beaded skirt and black tank top stood to greet them, pushing her long curly hair back over her shoulders.

"Mom, this is Kelly," Nick said. "Kelly, this is my mother."

"Call me Dinora," the woman said, offering Kelly her hand. She had colorful stones on most of her fingers.

"Pretty rings," Kelly said.

"Thanks. I designed this one and this one." She touched the ring on her forefinger and another ring on her left thumb. "It's very lovely to meet you, Kelly. Nick has told me . . ." She looked at her son and something seemed to pass between them that made her sigh. ". . . absolutely nothing about you."

"Mom," Nick protested.

"I'm not meddling. I'm not. I'm just pleased to see you're making friends. It's tough to be the new kid. I know that." Her gaze shifted to Kelly. "Isn't that right, Kelly?"

"I'm glad I never had to do it," Kelly said.

"Mom. We've been through this before. It's not like I need a ton of people around me—"

"Even sensitive artistic types need connection and belonging," Dinora said. "I worry about the way you tend to isolate yourself—"

"Uh, can we not do this in front of—"

"Ah," Dinora said, looking at Kelly, smiling in a way Kelly found charming, "my son is right. I can be careless about boundaries. Never know when to shut up. I think that's why Nick talks so little. Because he grew up with me talking so much."

"And I'm not a sensitive artistic type," Nick said. "I just swung by to pick up my gun and my football and a couple of six-packs."

"Nick feels he has to overcompensate for his sense of style," Dinora said and winked at Kelly. "For the fact that he has one. Some boys stash porn; Nick has *GQ* and *Esquire*."

"I have porn. You just haven't found it."

"And on that note of responsible parenting," Dinora said, "I'll give you two some privacy. Nick, just let me know what your plans are."

Nick nodded. Dinora smiled again at Kelly and moved past them into the hall and up the stairs, the skirt swishing around her legs.

"She should meet my mom," Kelly said. "I think they would really like each other. So—"

"Look." Nick scratched his neck and said, "My mom got wind of the thing and I told her I wouldn't go. That whole scene makes her kind of nervous."

Kelly grinned. "Awwww. And Nicky's a good boy? Always does what his mommy wants him to?"

She touched his shoulder playfully but he shrugged her off and she could see that she had genuinely annoyed him. "Look, my dad's not a good man, okay? The divorce has been really rough and I'm the man of the house now and I need to look out for her, you know?"

"Sure," Kelly said, although she wasn't really listening; she was too busy forming her argument. "And you *should* think about her. And you can think about her . . . tomorrow."

She was smiling at him and she touched his arm again. This time he didn't move away. He was smiling back at her and the way he looked in that moment—caught—made her feel dangerous and powerful, like the girl on one of those TV shows who was always luring boys into trouble. *Femme fatale*, her mother called them. Her mother said it was an archetype.

Nick said, "Tomorrow? So what about tonight?"

"You should think about me."

"About you."

"About what I need." She moved around him, ran her fingers lightly along the length of his spine.

"You're so evil," Nick said, then laughed.

"'Evil' is a strong word," Kelly said.

"Where did you learn to act like that, anyway?"

Kelly shrugged. "TV."

"The corrupting influence of television," Nick said. "Can you do that spine thing again?"

"No. May I get a drink?"

He led her across the hall and into the kitchen. It was small, with yellow cupboards that gave off the smell of fresh paint. Nick took a Coke from the fridge and handed it to her, saying, "So you still couldn't convince your brother to take you?"

"He's a traitor," Kelly muttered, cracking open the drink. The can was cold in her palm. She took greedy swallows, then ran the back of her hand across her mouth. "Thanks."

"No problem."

"He's a traitor," Kelly said again. "He knows I'll sneak out anyway, but when I asked him for a ride he just looked at me and said, 'Look, you screwed up. Deal with it.'" She was about to say something else, then paused. She was thinking about the way his gaze had drifted, as it so often did, to the faint tracings of scars around her mouth, to the larger scar along her cheek. The scars didn't bother her. She wished they'd quit bothering her brother. When she dabbed on a bit of makeup you couldn't even see them unless you knew where to look. But no matter how many years passed, Jasper always knew where to look. "He doesn't have to be a prig," Kelly said. "He's not my dad. I don't need another dad. He's my brother. He should just be cool."

Nick was leaning against the counter, loosely folding his arms, smiling at her. "Okay," he said. "Let's go."

The valley was spilling over. Cars were parked along the road and kids were streaming down the hillside into the sprawl of party below. A DJ was set up on the outdoor stage and the air thrummed with an electronic beat. Kelly grinned, grabbed Nick's hand. "The music doesn't suck," she said happily and Nick only looked at her and shook his head.

For a while they just wandered. Kelly figured she was probably one of the youngest people there and felt a thrill of pride. She recognized some kids from school, but the crowd slanted toward people in their twenties and there were a lot of the backpacker types who drifted through town on their way to someplace more interesting. The air was laced with cigarette smoke, the high sweet scent of marijuana.

One guy touched Nick on the arm and said something in

his ear. Nick only shrugged and glanced at Kelly. "You want to try a little E?"

"The guy's offering it to us?"

"Fifteen bucks a pill," the guy said. He was blond and clean-cut. Kelly had never met a drug dealer before—at least, not that she knew of—but she didn't know that they could look so . . . wholesome. "They're very good."

Kelly found herself dropping her voice, even though amid the swirl of crowd noise and music there was no possible way that anyone could hear them. She said to Nick, "Have you tried it before?"

Nick shrugged: either he didn't want to admit that he had or didn't want to admit that he hadn't. Kelly said, "I've never done it before. How about we just share one?"

"Sure, do a half each," the guy said. "But later on you'll want more."

Kelly pulled a ten-dollar bill from her pocket and managed to locate some ones and a handful of change in her knapsack. "Just one," she said.

The guy shrugged. "You'll just want more later. You'll have to come find me."

The pill was green, about the size of an aspirin but thicker. There was an image of an apple stamped in the middle.

"Just bite it in half," the guy said. "Give half to your boyfriend."

"He's not my—"

"Okay," Nick said. "Go ahead, Kel."

Kelly pulled a bottle of water from her knapsack and placed the pill between her teeth. She bit down hard, winced at the bitter, awful taste that flooded her mouth, then washed it down with water. She gave the jagged remainder to Nick.

"How long before it works?" Kelly said.

"Soon. Have fun, kids." The guy drifted off. Kelly saw him approach another couple, who listened a moment and then shook their heads.

Kelly and Nick walked and wandered and talked to people they knew and people they didn't and Kelly gradually began to realize that all of her tiredness was gone; she felt as alert and chatty as if she'd had a nap and a big cup of coffee. She had no idea what time it was; she had no sense of time passing at all. She couldn't seem to stop smiling. On impulse she slipped her arms around Nick's waist. He looked down at her and grinned and she grinned back at him and felt a wave of warmth and bliss wash deliciously through her; she just felt so good, so connected, so connected to Nick, and she said, "You know, I think I really like you," and Nick's face lit up and he laughed and he led her through the crowd and beyond to a thick gnarled oak. He took her behind it, where they were afforded a little pocket of privacy, and then they were kissing.

They were leaning against the tree, the bark scraping through her jacket, and kissing; then they were lying in the cool dewy grass, kissing, and Kelly had never realized that kissing could be so good. His hands were inside her jacket, then inside

her shirt, shockingly cold against her skin but getting warmer. She closed her eyes and laughed, she felt so good, and
hugged Nick as tightly as she could. But then something
strange happened. She had a weird sense of . . . separating
from herself . . . and for a moment she was standing way off
to the side of things, looking at two teenagers making out
beneath an oak tree, and she was saying to someone, *No,*
saying it to an animal of all things, *We were so into each other
like that because of that drug. There's nothing between us that's
real. Not yet.*

Dizziness swept over her then and she felt snapped back
inside her own body. She pulled away from Nick a little and
widened her eyes. "Something wrong?" Nick said, propping
himself up on his elbows.

"I just—"

She didn't want him touching her anymore. She got to
her feet with some effort; she wondered if she was going
to be sick. A tall man with bright pale hair stepped out of
the shadows farther along the hillside. He wore jeans and a
long pale coat. For some reason she couldn't take her eyes
off him.

"Kelly?" Nick was touching her arm.

The man was weaving through the crowd; he moved
with ease and grace, like he knew exactly where he was
going.

Nick said, "Kelly, you're looking kinda . . . shaky."

"There's no water left," she said, tipping the bottle. Her
throat had gone dry.

"Wait here. I'll find some."

Her vision seemed to have gone dim at the edges. Nick was there, then he was not there, and she wasn't sure how much time had passed since he had been not-there. The nausea and dizziness ebbed away and she felt so light—as if her bones had filled with helium—that she couldn't stop herself from rising and drifting into the crowd.

The bright-haired man snagged at the edge of her vision, but when she turned in his direction he wasn't anywhere. But Jasper was there, with his friends, laughing and drinking from a red plastic cup. He looked over and saw her and his expression swiftly changed. He was not pleased to see her there, Kelly realized; but she decided that she felt good enough for the both of them. "Hi, Jasper!" She grinned and waved with both hands.

He said something to his friends, then came over to her and grabbed her arm and pulled her into an opening at the side of the crowd where they could actually hear each other. "What the hell are you doing here? You're grounded."

"So what?"

"Kelly," he said, "what the hell . . . look at your *eyes*. Jesus Christ. Are you high?"

"No, no, no," she said and laughed.

"I don't believe this. What did you take?"

"Only half."

"Half of what? An E?"

"E is for ecstasy," she said and giggled again.

Jasper swore beneath his breath.

"Like you've never done it," Kelly snapped. The good feeling had ebbed a little.

"I don't do that shit, *any* of that shit, and you know it."

"Maybe you should." Her voice was a challenge. "You're so tense all the time. You should loosen up, lighten up. Maybe then you would lose that—that haunted, hunted look you carry around—"

"We need to get you home," Jasper said. "I'm taking you home."

"I'm not going home!"

"I'm not in the mood to babysit you, okay?"

"You don't need to babysit me! I'm a grown woman!"

"Wow. That's the funniest thing I've heard all night."

The world seemed to be going away from her a little; her vision felt punched in at the edges. She still felt good, but time seemed to be stopping and starting and stopping again. It was weird. She felt weird. Suddenly she realized she and Jasper were in a different part of the party and she had no memory of how they'd gotten there. "Just stay here, okay? Ronnie's got my jacket, my keys. I'll be right back, okay?"

But Kelly was already crawling into the back of the car. She just wanted to lie there and close her eyes and feel the world moving around her.

She was drifting off into a deep mellow feeling that wasn't quite sleep when car doors opened and a cool gust of wind touched her skin. "Jasper?" she said, or tried to say, when a male voice that wasn't her brother's said, "Look, I'll just drive you home and come right back and he won't even notice."

A girl responded, "You should maybe ask him first?"

"Sure, if I could find him."

The girl sighed. "I break curfew one more time, they won't let me go to Miami."

"Yeah, your parents are dicks."

"Ronnie!" the girl squealed.

"Look, you want to make curfew or not? It'll take five minutes. Jasper won't mind."

Doors opening, slamming. Fresh air sweeping in. The engine jumped to life. The girl said, "You okay to drive?"

"I'm fine."

"Maybe I should drive."

"You need to learn how to handle a stick, little girl."

"I love it when you talk dirty," the girl said. "Not."

Hey, I'm back here, Kelly said, or tried to say, *didn't Jasper find you? Didn't he tell you that I'm back here . . . ?* But although the words seemed to be hovering around her head she couldn't manage to reach out and grab them. Well, whatever. She closed her eyes. Things would turn out okay. Somebody else would make sure of that. Somebody always did.

The warm waves of the drug lifted her and when she opened her eyes again—*I should really let them know I'm back here*—Kira was chatting about a CD she liked. Then she said, "This isn't working."

"Sure it's working," Ronnie said.

"Either I am severely technologically challenged or this isn't working."

"Did you press the button?"

"I pressed several buttons."

Her head felt extremely heavy, but she was able to lift it

at least a few inches off the backseat. She was about to attempt actual speech when Kira screamed, "Look out!" and
the car whipped around as violently as a carnival ride, skid-
ding across the road. Through the car window Kelly saw the
deer standing in the middle of the road, head raised, looking
at them with wide eyes as if to say, "Who, me?"

And then—in her last moments of consciousness—Kelly
saw something that even in that still-stoned and terrified
moment she realized must be a hallucination, a phantom
from a dream: Because there was a girl in the road and her
face expressed all the horror that Kelly knew she should be
feeling but couldn't quite because everything was still so
beautiful, so blissful, as the car spun out of control and Kira
continued to scream and they flew off the edge of the road.
There was a girl in the road, and for that shocked heartbeat
of a moment, the two of them locked eyes, and the girl's eyes
were a familiar shade of blue. Her own.

CHAPTER TWENTY

The coyote said, *Remember now?*

Kelly spun around in surprise. She still thought she was in the back of the car—except she was here, sober as black coffee, on the side of the wooded road, with the coyote. Not just any coyote but the *talking* coyote, she reminded herself, and bit down hard on laughter that felt a bit hysterical.

Lights cut through the darkness and a car passed through the trees.

You're in that car, the coyote said and Kelly tried to adjust to the sense that she was divided in two: the present-tense Kelly who had somehow gone back in time, and the past-tense Kelly, still stoned in the back of a white car. *Do you remember what happened next?*

"There was an accident," Kelly said. "There was an accident—"

She was running out onto the road. There was a stirring

in a thicket and a deer flashed from the trees, the glow of its white tail in the dark just ahead of her. The car braked with a sharp squeal and slid sideways. The deer was gone as suddenly as it had appeared, the white of its tail bobbing into darkness. But the car was still spinning, the driver failing to get control of it. "No!" Kelly yelled. "No!" She made brief eye contact with the girl in the back of the car—a terrifyingly familiar blue-eyed girl—before the car hurled into the ravine. Kelly heard the loud horrible thumping sounds in the dirt as it crashed through bushes and undergrowth, as it found a resting place.

Then silence.

"I couldn't stop it," she yelled. "I was supposed to stop it and I couldn't. You brought me here for nothing—"

I didn't bring you here for that, the coyote said. *That was never within your power.*

She could hear the wind moving in the branches high above.

She whispered, "What do we do now?"

Wait.

"For what?"

Him.

Jasper was walking down the road.

The sky was turning into the soft pale shade of dawn. Jasper strode quickly, head down, hands in his pockets. He walked with urgency and purpose.

The coyote was silent, his gaze intent, his ears pricked.

Jasper stopped in his tracks. Even across the distance that separated them, Kelly could see the confusion and alarm that wrenched his features. He was looking in the direction of the fallen car. Then he was running—his feet slapping off the dirt road, slipping in the gravel, as he half-slid his way down into the ditch.

Now is the time for a new perspective, the coyote said.

Kelly felt a cool rush of air. They were standing in a different spot in the woods. Now Kelly could see straight into the ravine: the car flipped onto its side and smashed against a thicket of trees. The windshield was broken and stained with blood. She covered her eyes, took a breath, then dropped her hand and looked again. There was a girl sitting with her back against a tree and Jasper was crouched in front of her.

The girl was her.

Past-tense Kelly.

"Jasper," Archie said.

He had appeared on the road above the ravine. Jasper looked up at the sound of his voice and yelled, "Call nine-one-one! Do it now!"

"Sorry." Archie's voice was deadly soft. "I don't do that."

Jasper looked at him again. The wind itself seemed to stop blowing, the whole wood held its breath. Jasper said, in a strange flat voice Kelly had never heard him use before, "Oh. It's you."

"It's been a long time, Jasper."

"Yeah. I'd almost convinced myself you weren't real. Just a bogeyman."

"But I'm so much prettier than that."

"What do you want?"

"I want to help you. Jasper, Jasper. She's dying, Jasper."

"You don't know that!"

"Head wound," Archie said. "And it's all your fault."

"Ronnie's a decent guy," Jasper said. "I don't under-stand how— He hadn't been— How could this have hap-pened?"

"Remember the dog, Jasper? When she wandered away to pet the mean old dog? She was on your watch. Remember the look in your parents' eyes? How do you think they'll look at you this time?"

"Stop talking," Jasper said. He raised his hands to his head. "Stop talking."

"I can change this for you, if you like. Your parents will never have to look at you that way again."

"I don't believe you."

"Don't you know what I am? Haven't you figured it out yet?"

"You're the devil," Jasper whispered.

"Don't be so dramatic." Archie tipped his head. "Tell you what I'll do. I'll get an ambulance here quicker than quick. Give you some time to think things over. I'll get back to you."

I was coming out of the hospital . . . they were waiting for me. They had a bike for me. All I had to do was get on it and ride.

"No," Kelly said. She lifted her voice. "Jasper! No! This has to end now!"

He can't hear you, the coyote said. *Remember, you're a ghost.*

Jasper showed no sign of hearing her.

But Archie did.

His head turned in her direction and they held gazes for what felt an endless moment, the wind shivering new breath through the leaves.

"You," Archie said. "How . . . ? It's that damn animal, isn't it? Where is he?" He looked around. The coyote was nowhere in sight. "Inigo!" Archie hollered. "Inigo! Come out and face me like a *man,* you damn dog!" He looked at Kelly. "Maybe I'll make a nice jacket out of him. In your size, maybe. My gift to you. Would you like that?"

"What's going on?" Jasper said. "Who are you talking to?"

"Jasper," Kelly said, but her brother's gaze remained on Archie.

"Talking to nobody," Archie said and waved a hand dismissively. "A ghost. Less than a ghost."

"I'm no goddamn ghost." Kelly felt the weight of her knapsack drag against her shoulders. She swung it around and zipped it open. She groped for the scissors. Any weapon was better than nothing. But what she pulled out was the painted stake from her memorial, the piece she'd picked up as a souvenir and put in her knapsack and forgotten about. Part of her own ruined creation that, in this particular moment, she hadn't even made yet. What could she do with something like this? Even the scissors would be better. Yet . . . it fitted so neatly against her palm like that. Her fingers curled around the smooth length. It felt like part of her. She was moving now, climbing up the ditch, and Archie showed no notice; either she was as invisible to him as she was to her brother or he was too focused on her brother to be aware of anything, anyone else. Except then his head turned slowly, his eyes, now so innocent and crystalline blue, widening, and he said, "Wait a minute—you're not supposed to—"

"You're just a stupid soul-sucking vampire," Kelly said and before he could react she had plunged the stake into his chest. It went in with surprising ease, as if piercing cardboard paper: there was a thin crust of resistance and then—nothing. It was so easy that she couldn't believe it had actually done any damage and yet he was staggering back several steps and looking at her in genuine shock, as if he'd been shot.

Everything stopped. The wind in the trees; the rustling leaves; even Jasper himself: it was as if the world had been plunged into freeze-frame.

Archie was looking at the stake in his chest, at the large thickly lashed eye painted along the side, staring back at him in accusation or disbelief or maybe a weird form of sympathy.

He lifted his gaze to Kelly.

"I'm not sure what you mean to accomplish by this," he said.

"You can't have him. I won't let you."

"You? *You* won't let me?" He laughed, but Kelly saw something flit through his eyes—concern, she thought. Worry. He was staring intently at her, but she refused to look away. Jasper's words came back to her. "You have to stare right into the abyss. You have to have the mental strength."

"You're it," she whispered softly. "You're the void. The abyss. That's what you are. That's all you are."

"You realize you die here, Kelly." But there was an edge to his voice. He was worried, she saw. Things were not going as planned. She was meddling in ways he could not have anticipated. "Do you really want to die for your brother?"

"You lie," Kelly said. "You'll say anything."

"Oh for the love of . . . okay, if you want to get technical. So maybe you *don't* die. At least not at once. Maybe it takes months. Or maybe years." He shrugged—and then winced, as if the gesture hurt him. He scowled at the stake, gingerly tried to extract it.

She grabbed the stake with her hand, preventing him from withdrawing it any farther. She expected him to laugh and shrug her away . . . and yet he didn't. Couldn't. She kept staring into his eyes.

The wood remained embedded in his body, jutting from his pale coat. There was no blood, she noticed. How come there wasn't any blood?

"Nick was right," she said. "You're nothing." No wonder the stake had gone in so easily. "That's why you have to make your bargains. Because you can't do what people won't *let* you."

His eyes were blazing. "I'm not," he said. "Haven't you felt the shadow of it all along? That abyss is for you, Kelly. That's what I saved you from. And maybe you'll wake up, maybe one day, but maybe you'll linger on for years and years and *then* finally die. Is that what you want?"

She said, with an acid in her voice that surprised her, "No matter how it turns out, I'll still have my soul, won't I?"

He considered her for a long moment. He was a tall thin figure with impossibly long legs and a bright thatch of hair, his long-fingered hands wrapped around the hilt of the stake jutting from his coat. His eyes had turned vivid and purple and Kelly thought she caught something in them that might have been respect, if the most grudging kind.

"You're more interesting than I realized," he allowed.

"Go back," Kelly said. "Go home."

And he looked at her with a deep sadness in his eyes.

"I can't," he said. Then: "Let me do this. Save you, save him. Let me do just this one little thing."

"No," Kelly said and pushed the stake into him with all the strength in her body. "I'd rather die."

He fell to his knees, never taking his eyes off her. She didn't look away. Her chest hurt. She gasped, gulped at the air. Archie's eyes changed from purple to bright red to a darker blood-red and then to brown, the soft questioning brown of a hound dog's eyes. "I was only trying to help you," Archie whispered. "All of you."

And then, in a sharp flat sound like ripping paper, he disappeared into a cloud of black mist. Kelly saw something boiling inside it, something moving and fluttering. A horde of creatures small, black, and winged exploded from the inky haze and streaked in all directions, some of them straight toward Kelly. She cried out and covered her head with her arms. There was a high, keening, chittering sound and she opened one eye to catch blurred glimpses of the creatures, saw feathery wings and strangely shaped heads and vivid eyes in all colors of the rainbow—

And then they were gone.

The last of the creatures followed its kindred, spiraling up into the sky, and the sky itself seemed to open up and swallow them whole.

Her legs were trembling so badly it was impossible to stand. Kelly let herself collapse into the dead leaves, the earth cold beneath her, but half a moment later she was forcing herself to get back up. She picked her way over to where her brother was still caught inside this freeze-frame moment, staring ashen-faced at the past-tense Kelly. Kelly kneeled beside him, reached out, and touched the face of this other version of herself.

She felt herself merging; felt these split versions of herself coming together, like a wound finally healing. There was a dull heavy pain in her head and she could feel blood trickling past her ear, but none of that mattered. "You're safe," she told her brother, because the world was moving forward again. The rich smells of the wood and the jagged sound of Jasper's breathing came at her with new urgency. Speaking was difficult, but she needed to tell her brother something before she went down into the dark. "You're safe now," she said.

"Kelly—"

But her gaze had gone behind him to see something else. A door had materialized in the air, a white hospital door, numbered 432. It was opening and she was going into it. And that was okay. That was fine.

"It will all be okay," Kelly said. She closed her eyes.

EPILOGUE

Kelly Ruland was dreaming of a coyote.

She was following him through rooms and more rooms in a house that was constantly changing.

She saw a blur of gray light, white walls, a dingy yellow curtain hanging around her bed. Someone pulled it back, curtain rings rattling. *Nurse,* Kelly thought. *So I must be in a hospital.* For some reason this didn't surprise her, although she couldn't think of why she might be here. Her memory felt like a windswept canyon, nothing there but echoes.

"Oh my dear," the nurse said and just before Kelly felt her eyelids closing again, she saw the coyote sitting in the far corner of the room. He had something in his mouth. He lowered his head and dropped it on the floor.

Kelly went away again.

*   *   *

Voices kept drifting down to her. Sometimes she let them wash over her; sometimes she followed them up to the surface, back to the gray light and the curtain and people in white uniforms coming in and out. Things became a little more in focus, as if someone crouched behind her eyes and kept adjusting the lens. Faces hovered. Friends from school, toting the bright shapes of balloons and flowers. Her parents. She was able to smile at them. Her mother was crying. Her father said something that might have been, *Hanging tough, kiddo, that's my girl.* She felt herself sinking again. But that was okay, that was fine; the voices, the light, her family would still be there when she felt strong enough to surface again. Strong enough to stay.

She opened her eyes and Jasper was sitting there. He was reading a magazine.

Her voice felt like an ancient artifact. She had to work to unearth it. "Hi," she croaked and Jasper's head jerked up as if he'd been shot.

"Hi!" he said. "Hi there!" He sprang off his chair, hovered over her, smiling. For some reason she'd been expecting him to be really skinny, gaunt-faced, but he was just the normal, healthy Jasper she remembered.

He said, "Are you back for good, do you think?"

"Yeah," she said and already it was getting easier to speak.

*   *   *

Some time later, in one of the spaces of peace and quiet between visitors and tests and physical therapy and meal service and conversations with doctors and nurses, when she was alone again with her brother, he brought his chair close to the bed and said, "What was it like?"

She had been in a coma for almost a year. The idea gave her a weird feeling in her stomach, as if she was standing at the edge of the Grand Canyon. She'd lost a year of her life. Gone. Her mother—her pregnant mother, yet another impossible fact to wrap her mind around, her mother's belly just beginning to take on the rounded shape beneath the loose silk tunics she favored—had brought Kelly a hand mirror at Kelly's request. It lay on the bedside table and Kelly kept stealing glances at this strange girl in the mirror: older, paler, thinner.

"What was it like?" she said now, echoing Jasper's question as if asking it of herself. She settled against the pillows, swinging aside the little tray table that held the remains of her lunch. "A lot of dreams," she said finally. "That's what I remember. A lot of strange dreams."

"What did you dream about?"

"You," she said immediately. "And . . . other things."

A strange sad smile crossed Jasper's face and for a moment he looked about a thousand years old.

"A talking coyote," he said, "and a man with wings?"

She stared at him.

"What did you say?" she said and he repeated the words she thought she had heard, but still couldn't believe.

She said, "How could you know that?"

Outside it was late spring, the sun bouncing off the cars in the parking lot. She wanted to be out there, in the light and breezy warmth. She wanted to go to the shopping mall and see a movie and sit in the food court and eat a cheeseburger.

Soon, the doctor had promised her.

"How could I know that?" Jasper echoed. There was a bleakness in his eyes she didn't know how to interpret. "I have some strange dreams of my own."

"Yeah? Like what?"

He shrugged.

"Tell me," she said.

"I dreamed I rode with a really strange bunch of guys. We would fly down the highway and the light turned all golden and sometimes we weren't even . . . sometimes we weren't even on the ground."

"Flying," Kelly said.

"It felt like that."

"It sounds wonderful."

"It was, at first. But the longer it went on, the more you felt yourself turning into a ghost. Like nothing you did or said could ever matter. Like you didn't even belong to yourself anymore. Like you weren't connected to anything outside of . . . the ride." He shifted in the chair. She thought maybe he would refuse to continue, but he surprised her. "We'd camp out at motels or in the fields or in strangers' houses, whether they wanted us there or not. Our leader—I guess you could call him that—was this guy with really blond hair."

"And wings," Kelly said. "He had wings."

"He had a friend," Jasper said. "*We* weren't his friends. We were more like his possessions. But he had this animal who would drop by from time to time and you'd see them going off on long walks together. Sometimes they'd be gone a few days. But one day the guy came back alone. He said the coyote was dead and we should never ask about him again."

"But that's not what happened," Kelly said.

"I investigated," Jasper said. "I found him in a bar."

"He was in a bar?"

"He was in a cage being kept in the back. Like a kind of sideshow. Freak show. He was miserable. I asked him why he couldn't escape on his own and he told me he had no power over iron."

"You talked to him?"

"Of course not. That's impossible," Jasper said. "But I went and got some tools and came back at night when the owner was gone and broke into the place and managed to take apart the cage. So the coyote was free. He was pretty grateful. He gave me some good advice about where to go next, who to see. And he said he'd help me any way he could. He owed me."

"Nice dream," Kelly said.

"Sure. What would Freud say, do you think?"

"Probably the same thing: 'Nice dream.'"

"Yeah," Jasper said. They swapped smiles.

*   *   *

When she was packing up to go home, planning to donate the stuffed animals to the children's wing, she found the small thing on her windowsill.

It was a chunk of wood, rough and splintery, and there was something painted on it: a woman's eye, the same shape and shade of blue as her own. A tiny hole had been drilled in the wood and a leather cord looped through it. Something flitted at the edge of Kelly's memory, swooping and elusive as a ghost. She felt a bone-deep chill, as if that ghost had blown right through her.

The memorial, she thought. *It got ruined.*

Her mind flashed on the image of some kind of structure in the woods, a tall obelisk made out of wood, and for a moment she was convinced it had existed, that she had even made it with a friend of hers—with Nick, the new boy at school who was very cute and seemed a little shy but had kissed her at the rave. Nick was her friend, she realized suddenly, a really *good* friend, turning into a *boy*friend . . . except she didn't really know him, did she? And the memorial had never existed.

She remembered the coyote she had followed through her coma dreams. She remembered how, for the briefest of moments, she had watched him sitting in the corner of this very hospital room. How he'd had something in his mouth. How he had dropped it. Someone else must have found it, figured it for a thing she might want to keep, and placed it on the windowsill.

"Trickster," she heard herself murmur. "Boundary crosser."

She thought, *And maybe I am, too.*

She slipped the cord around her neck and held the piece of wood against her palm like a talisman.

Jasper took her out to the movies. They saw a movie with Johnny Depp: "He's still really hot," Kelly said when the actor first came on screen, "even if he is kind of old. So at least *that* hasn't changed," and Jasper laughed.

Afterward they got cheeseburgers and found a table in the food court. Kelly kept looking around at the women rushing past with shopping bags, the mannequins standing inside front windows displaying fall fashions, the suburban teenage boys dressed like rappers, stuffing their mouths with French fries. It was very noisy—voices refracting off the walls, the ceiling, and skylight, until they seemed to be bouncing off each other—but she didn't mind. She was alive and awake and could hear Jasper just fine.

He had decided not to go to Harvard, he explained. "I couldn't. Not after what happened to you. It felt wrong."

"Wrong? You mean, like, morally?"

"More like inauthentic. False. Like going to Harvard and being a doctor was just this part I'd been playing, you know, because it was a good answer to give people when they asked me certain questions. Because the truth is, when I went to visit the campus? I didn't even like the place very much. I just couldn't see myself living there, *being* there." Instead, he had worked and traveled. "I'd go to India for a few weeks, come back home, spend time with the parents and you at the hospital, work at the restaurant, then go to Thailand for a few weeks . . . I did a lot of thinking and writing. I guess what you'd call soul-searching."

He was going to NYU in the fall. He wanted to be a writer.

"What did Dad say when you told him this?"

"After what was going on with you? Jesus, Kelly, I could have told him I wanted to run off to Vegas and be a male stripper and he would have nodded and said, 'Whatever makes you happy, son.'"

"So you'll be in New York," Kelly said. "Living in the city."

"You should come and visit as often as you can. It'll be good for you. Expand your horizons."

"You'll be leaving me at home all alone," Kelly said. "Just me and the parentals. And Mojo."

Jasper grinned wickedly. "And the twins."

"The *twins*," Kelly said, and groaned. Another Grand Canyon fact of life to deal with: her mother wasn't just pregnant, she was pregnant with twins. What's more, Hannah had informed them over dinner last night that she would have to go on bed rest soon. Kelly could not imagine someone like her mother forced to stay in bed for weeks, *months,* on end. Hannah was going to go nuts, which just might drive them all nuts.

Jasper said, "Don't look so worried, Kel."

"I'm not worried."

"It's going to be fine."

"I know that," Kelly said and Jasper reached across the table and gave her arm a squeeze.

Later, when they had stepped onto the escalator and were gliding down toward the exit, Kelly said, "Do you still have those dreams?"

Jasper didn't answer. He was looking over the side of the escalator, into the crowd below.

"Jasper?"

"What?" He turned too quickly. His face had gone pale, she noticed . . . except then he smiled and seemed okay. "Sorry," he said. "What was that?"

"Do you still have those dreams?"

He shrugged. "It's a strange world, Kel, getting stranger all the time. You learn how to deal." Which wasn't the yes-or-no answer she'd been expecting, but seemed a good answer all the same.

As they stepped off the escalator and walked past the stone fountain, coins winking up through the water, Kelly felt a breath of warm air on the back of her neck. She stopped. Turned. Wondered if she'd stepped into some kind of weird draft, except all she felt now was the air-conditioned briskness that filled the mall.

Then, toward the back of the ground floor, where the boutiques gave way to the entrance of the adjoining grocery store, she caught a glimpse of a tall bright-haired man moving through the crowd. He was there, then gone, and she couldn't account for the eel of a feeling slipping down around her bones. He was just some guy, after all, just some stranger she'd never seen before—

Except she knew him. She even knew his name.

"Archie," she whispered.

Your soul's turning deeper and richer all the time, sweet Kelly. Maybe we'll meet up again, who can tell? Like your brother just told you, it's a strange world, this one, and only getting stranger.

She stumbled. "Hey," Jasper said, grabbing her shoulder to steady her. "Hey, what happened?"

She was scanning the crowds, looking for that flash of pale hair, listening for a voice that seemed to speak from the very air.

"He's out there," she said.

She expected Jasper to say "Who?" except he didn't. Didn't have to.

"Oh," Jasper said instead, scorn in his voice, "he always is." He made a gesture with his hand. "And so are scorpions, rattlesnakes, man-eating sharks. Lots of dangerous creatures out there. You learn how to deal."

They reached the heavy glass doors, and then they were pushing through them into the warmth and the light.